NEW YORK
STATE OF MIND

A NOVEL BY
BRIAN ROGERS

New York State of Mind

Published by: R and R Publishing, LLC
Cover Design by: Davida Baldwin

ISBN: 978-0-9824598-0-5

For all correspondences and inquiries email us at:
randrpublishingllc@gmail.com

Be sure to visit us online at:

www.NewYorkStateOfMindBook.com

Printed in the United States of America

Acknowledgements

First, I would like to thank my wife, Naeisha, for giving me the support and encouragement that helped me to fulfill my passion of writing and for allowing me to be me.

I would also like to thank my two sons, Duvon and Lil' Brian, for inspiring me to be the best person that I can be. You motivate me and give my life a greater meaning.

My mother and father, I thank you for instilling my values and principles that helped to shape and mold me into the person I am today. Grams, I love you. You are the personification of a REAL grandmother. My baby sister, Deveny, thank you for all the support and for truly being my best friend. To my cousins Tammy, Tasha, Keithy, and Sheena, thank you for starting off so good transcribing my manuscript from my sometimes illegible writing.

Thanks to all my friends and associates who give me support in various ways to help me distribute this book to different outposts all over the world.

Last but certainly not least, I would like to thank all of the people who purchased this book. Your support is greatly appreciated.

Much Love,

Brian Rogers

Chapter 1

Rimzy Brown looked at the simple calendar on the wall and read the date aloud to himself. "May 10, 2011," he said with an anticipatory smirk, "the beginning of the summer!" Rimzy couldn't believe that on this very date, he was finally coming home at the ripe age of 27. As he waited for his cell door to open for the final time, he caught a flashback.

He imagined grey walls, grey floors, grey ceilings, grey bars...all dinged, drab, dense and dark. He pictured himself waking up to this pathetic existence day in and day out without basic freedoms and being constantly robbed of all dignity. This was the very nightmare that Rimzy, ironically, had woken up to every day for seven years. Arising to that nightmare was something terrible for Rimzy, but this was his last morning in that 'chamber of doom.' Today was the day of all days–his release day.

As Rimzy sat in his cell enduring the last few minutes of captivity before his impending release, his mind drifted back to his journey to Sing Sing. He remembered sitting pensive on the transport bus as it made its rounds dropping off prisoners at various correctional facilities. With each stop Rimzy grew more optimistic. Prisoners disembarked to facilities with sprawling manicured grass grounds and even gardens here and there, and he was reminded of some college campuses he had seen in passing while he was still free. He thought, for a second, that the experience could perhaps be pleasant. Then, the bus pulled up to his stop and Rimzy was instantly sickened. There was no mistaking Sing Sing for what it was; one of the worst correctional facilities in the state of New York. It was called a "disciplinary max jail," meaning some of the most dangerous prisoners in the state were held therein.

Sing Sing was known to many as 'Gladiator School.' The unwelcoming correctional facility was a place that seemed like it was made to break spirits, and it had done so more than once. From the moment he saw the 200-foot dark grey wall that surrounded the prison with guard towers situated on top, Rimzy sensed that he was in the big league; though he was largely unaware of the extent to which he would become engulfed by the never-ending tension that rested inside.

Rimzy was taken aback by the sight of Sing Sing. His life at that point in time seemed to be unraveling much like a scene right out of the movies. As the bus went through each of seven heavy fences Rimzy felt as if the weight of these metal enclosures was not only closing him in, but also closing in on him. They entered next to the prison yard which was the size of twenty football fields. For a split second, Rimzy juxtaposed the immensity of the yard with immensity of the situation facing him, but there was no comparison.

Rimzy stepped off of the bus like it was a slave ship. It wasn't an easy task since he was bound and shackled. His hands were cuffed, and the cuffs were placed in a black box that restricted any movement of the wrist. The box had a hole in it that was connected to a chain wrapped twice around his waist. This further restricted any movement of his wrists, hands, and arms. One of his feet was fettered to that of another prisoner, and it took careful precision for them to complete even the simplest task. Every movement had to be synchronized between shackled prisoners. In an instant their individuality was diminished as they were forced to become one, due to the simple yet debilitating fact that any movement not coordinated would result in the small chain getting the better of them. As Rimzy took calculated steps, he marveled at how well such a contraption served its purpose of both literally and figuratively containing so many men within little black boxes.

Once Rimzy and his ankle partner made it safely from the bus to the reception area, they encountered eight brawny corrections officers. This confirmed his intuition, which had suggested that life was going to be real inside of Sing Sing. Rimzy had just finished doing two years in Upstate, a Special Housing Facility commonly referred to as the box, where he was locked in his cell for 23 hours a day. He was placed in the box for cutting another prisoner and knocking out a corrections officer. He had lost a considerable amount of weight in the Box, and weighed about 150 pounds. Accordingly, he looked incredibly fragile in his state-issued uniform, which was mandated when prisoners were on a draft, being transferred to another facility. The uniform consisted of standard pants, sweatshirt, state coat, and state hat, all of which were green. The only personal item Rimzy had was his specs which were modeled after Malcolm X's trademark sleek black glasses, giving him a semi-sophisticated look. Nonetheless, this get-up was totally inadequate for traveling on a 12-degree February day. Just moving from the bus to the reception area, the cold on the outside left him feeling almost as cold and numb as he felt on the inside.

As soon as Rimzy and the other few remaining prisoners were ushered into the reception area, they were lined up, while the transit officers removed their shackles. Before they even had a chance to stretch, three corrections officers from Sing Sing immediately placed their own handcuffs on them. They were subsequently ushered into a holding pen.

A few big, very intimidating officers made a show of skillfully brandishing and twirling their batons, demonstrating just how skillful they were at using them. Once the transit officers left, it was on. Two of the officers walked by the holding pen while ice grilling the prisoners, some of which turned their heads.

When Rimzy, who was fresh out of the Box and whose spirit was not yet broken, returned the glare, one of the officers said, "Let's do him first."

Eight officers stood outside of the holding pen grasping their sticks tightly, while one told Rimzy to step outside. He reluctantly obeyed.

Though his feet were no longer shackled Rimzy still took slow calculated steps, giving himself time to size up the officers. He gathered that the tallest most physically imposing guard that had barked the command was presumably running the show. Rimzy also realized that he would soon be made into an example for the other prisoners, and therefore the star of the impending jailhouse show.

The officer in charge coolly stated: "I'm getting ready to un-cuff you. As soon as you feel the metal removed from your wrists, you better put your hands in your pockets as fast as possible. If I feel you're not moving fast enough, I'm going to consider that an act of aggression, and me and my brothers are going to beat you unconscious."

As soon as they took off the cuffs, Rimzy did as he was told. Two of the officers gave each other a dirty look that Rimzy caught before they ushered him off to the side of the bullpen in plain view of the other prisoners.

When he got there, he saw a wall with a set of handprints and on the floor were a set of footprints. One officer stood on each side of Rimzy, holding their batons like baseball players awaiting the pitch. The charge officer stood behind and continued with his orders, instructing Rimzy to put his feet and hands on the imprints.

At 6'1", Rimzy thought, *how the hell am I going to reach the hand imprints when the foot imprints are crazy far from the wall?* He estimated it was a close call, but if he stretched to his fullest capacity he should make it; and he did...barely. The awkward position left him vulnerable and off balance. The same officer then told him to slowly remove his left hand from the wall in order to take off his right boot. Rimzy suddenly had a flashback of when he used to play Twister as a child. It probably wouldn't have been a hard move were he playing Twister, but this was not a game at all. In fact, with two officers standing nearby with batons, Rimzy was sure that things were quite serious, and in turn he began sweating bullets.

After complying to the next set of commands Rimzy stood in the same position adorned in nothing but socks. The officer then asked, "Where did you come from?"

"Upstate," Rimzy responded.

"Oh, the Box, huh? You must be a tough guy. Are you a tough guy?"

Rimzy thought to himself, *if we were in my hood in the Bronx, I would show you how tough I am,* but he wisely responded, "No, I am not a tough guy."

The C.O. behind him asked, "What did you do to go to the Box?"

Unbeknownst to Rimzy, the officers had already looked at his file before they took him out of the holding pen. So, they already knew he assaulted another officer, and had decided they were going to make an example out of him to set fear in the other prisoners who looked on closely. They were on some real psychological bullshit. Rimzy again felt like he had hopped off of the slave ship and on to the plantation. Like back in the day, when most slave owners were semi-literate lowlifes, and had to use 'Willie Lynch papers' as their blueprints on how to break and maintain their slave. Somehow these correctional officers revised the Willie Lynch papers and instead of separating the men from the women and doing public beatings, and so on, they separated Rimzy from his manhood and wield their sticks freely upon him in the privacy of their jail. Internally Rimzy though, *I guess these are the modern day slave drivers*…Then sinking back into the realness of the moment he responded simply: "I assaulted another prisoner." This was partly true.

He didn't want to tell the officers that he had also assaulted one of their own. Truth be told, he knocked one of them the fuck out. However, he wasn't about to tell those C.O.'s that bit of information. He had already got the ass whipping of a lifetime in Green Point for that shit.

The C.O. behind him asked, "Is that all?"

"Yes," Rimzy responded.

Right after the word left his mouth, one of the C.O.'s on the side of him hauled off and smacked him so hard, it felt like flames flew out of his mouth. His glasses went flying off his face, and the last thing he remembered before blacking out was attempting to reach for the officer who smacked him. By the time Rimzy became cognizant again, he was waking up in a single-man holding cage with his ribs, shins, shoulders, and back hurting. What a welcoming party.

Rimzy snapped out of his recollection and looked around his empty cell, which was devoid of all the prison luxuries that helped ease the pain of being confined to such a controlled environment. His walkman, headphones, tapes, hot pot, trimmers, fan, burgundy sheets and towels, clothing, shoes, and short eyes (girly books) were all given away to the unfortunate souls who had more time in the "chamber of doom". The only thing he sent home before his departure was his pictures and black history books.

Rimzy didn't waste much time with goodbyes as there were already so few that he associated with. While he prepared to leave, his two boys came through and told him to hold it down and to please stay free because this shit is not where it's at. Other people from the gallery sent their regards, though most were phony. Rimzy didn't have a lot of friends in Sing Sing. He intermingled only with a selected few, and still of all those in Rimzy's inner circle, he considered an even smaller amount like brothers to him.

After about an hour of sitting and anticipating, the sweetest sound of all sounds commenced; his cell door opened. Rimzy stepped out of his cell, B-Block, and walked down the gallery, through the gate that led to the steps, and proceeded down to the A-Block.

Before he left, he stopped at his good friend Crime's cell, where he was on keep lock. Crime stayed locked in twenty-three hours a day and was only allowed out for his court-mandated one-hour free period. Rimzy kicked it with Crime for a second before telling him to stay strong, and that he would keep in touch. Rimzy then proceeded to the rotunda that connected the A, B, C, and D Blocks. Once there, he stood on the wall and waited for the C.O. in the hallway to tell the one in the control room, which was often referred to as the bubble, to open the gate. Rimzy stood next to the bubble anticipating traveling down the final long hallway that led to freedom.

Rimzy felt the exhilaration rush through him as he began to take his last few steps on the long journey to freedom. But suddenly, an alarm started blaring, the gates locked shut, and Rimzy heard "RED DOT, RED DOT IN D BLOCK!" over one of the correction officer's walkie talkie. Next thing, the gates opened and about thirty C.O.'s came running to D Block. Then, the gates closed back. After about five minutes, Rimzy heard "RED DOT UNDER CONTROL," and about two minutes later, three C.O.'s and a sergeant came rushing by with a Spanish kid handcuffed and holding a towel to his face with massive blood dripping from it. They were undoubtedly taking him to the infirmary. About five minutes later, Rimzy saw his man Fire come through with eight C.O.'s and a sergeant. One officer was holding his handcuffed hands up as far as physically possible, while another one had his hand firmly planted on his back. Two others were on each side of him, holding his shoulders, while four more covered the front and back of the passing entourage. As Fire passed Rimzy, he looked up, smiled, and told him what he had already heard three times that day: "Don't come back."

Rimzy waited another twenty minutes before the C.O. finally gave the signal for the gate to be opened. The C.O. really thought he was doing something special by denying a man his freedom for the little bit of time he could. *What a mentality*, Rimzy thought to himself. As much as Rimzy wanted to get out, he didn't sweat the delay. The last thing he was going to do was let the C.O. think he had any control over him mentally. If it was one thing Rimzy learned over the seven years he was incarcerated, it was patience. He waited 2,559 days and 20 minutes, and it didn't break him. So, those last few minutes were a piece of cake.

He stood tall with his back up against the wall and his dark, rich skin glowing with its ebony shine for all of two minutes, before the gate opened and the officer in the rotunda motioned for Rimzy to walk through the gate. You didn't have to tell Rimzy twice, or in this case, motion twice by the time the guard looked up from releasing the gate opening mechanism, Rimzy was already walking down the corridor to another gate with a C.O. at a desk.

After the C.O. opened the gate, Rimzy walked to the package room and handed over his ID. The C.O. checked it against a black and white picture of Rimzy, then handed him a box while instructing him to change in the visiting room. Rimzy took the box, walked to the visiting room, and quickly changed out of his state clothes and into a sky blue Sean John short set with a pair of matching uptown sneakers that his mother had sent two weeks prior. After he dressed, he came back out and waited by the package room for ten more minutes, before the C.O. finished his important conversation about hunting deer and gave Rimzy two twenty-dollar bills, a bus ticket, and a check for $1,800.00, all of which remained in his inmate account.

Once Rimzy signed a receipt for those items, the C.O. at the desk got up from reading his paper to open yet another gate. Rimzy walked a little further to a door where a C.O. in another bubble buzzed the door, and Rimzy found himself standing in a little reception area.

Rimzy looked at the clock, which read 9:30 a.m. Then, he walked through two sets of swinging doors and was outside...and also a FREE MAN!

He took in the fresh warm air and thought to himself that summer 2011 was going to be his.

Chapter 2

There is an old convict saying that goes, "The air is cleaner on the other side of the wall." The wall must have had some type of stale prison air radiating off of it. It must have been some type of physiological illusion imbedded into his subconscious, because he could have sworn the yard never smelled this fresh.

Rimzy came out of his daze to the sound of familiar voices shouting his name. He looked in the direction of the voices and saw his two cousins in front of a decent-looking Maxima. Black and Blue were brothers. Blue had just come home from 3 tours of duty in Iraq. Black was an up and coming rapper who worked as a security guard. They could all three pass for brothers, because they were all about the same height, sharing the same muscular build, along with the same chocolate skin tone. Black was the first to get at Rimzy with a big hug. As soon as he finished, Blue was at his side to do the same.

After the love was distributed, Rimzy looked at them, and without looking back, he said, "Let's get the fuck out of here."

Black jumped into the driver's seat, Rimzy in the passenger's side, and Blue in the back. The car was left running, and Raekwon's classic "Only Built 4 Cuban Linx" was knocking on the system. They drove down a road that had beat up farmhouses with no animals. Actually, Putnam County was one of the poorest counties in New York. Prisons were the economy for a lot of small upstate towns.

When they got to the third intersection, Rimzy told Black to pull over so he could go to the bank and cash the check the facility had given him. It seemed like when Rimzy walked into the bank, all eyes were on him. He stepped to the window and presented the teller with the check, his birth certificate, and his social security card. These were the only pieces of identification he had, but it was all he needed for now, just as the pre-release people told him. He sent away for them, and they held the documents with his personal property until his release. The teller counted out the money and slid it to Rimzy.

As soon as he got back in the whip, he told Black, "Stop at the Nike outlet that everybody kept telling me about when they came to see me."

After pulling up at the outlet, which was about ten blocks from the bank, the three cousins stepped up in the spot with that city swagger that seemed to have all of those hillbilly rednecks fascinated. Rimzy snatched up a pair of throwback Jordan's and a pair of ACG boots, which he needed since his man Shabazz had a construction collision company he planned to get down with. He also copped a beige Nike sweat suit with a black racing stripe going down the side, along with a pair of shorts and a t-shirt.

Rimzy was down for a minute, seven years to be exact, but he kept up with the styles through the *Source*, *Vibe*, and a few other urban publications. He was always a fly dude, so it wasn't hard for him to coordinate a couple of outfits. He still got his cousins' approval of the gear he picked out, because after all, they were the ones who told him people weren't wearing creases in their pants anymore. The shit he copped wasn't anything major, but the clothes were something different. Rimzy hated to be walking down the avenue or up in the club and see somebody, or worst three or four people, wearing the same fashions he had on.

After taking the items to the counter, he was surprised to see a little brown-skinned cutie at the register. This being his first time seeing a honey since being released, he had to test his skills. So, he hit her with a smile, and she smiled back. Under different circumstances, he would've told himself he got her, but he realized she may have been just being polite because she was working.

After his quick analysis, he hit her with, "Hello, love. Let me ask you a question that has my mind boggled. What is a cutie like yourself doing up in these mountains?"

The question seemed appropriate seeing as how she was the only black person he saw in the whole outlet.

"I just work over here. I live in Albany," she replied.

"I know some people out there. I come through there every now and then. Next time I come through, do you think me and you could link up?" he asked, while peeling off a few Benjamin's.

"Where you from?" she asked.

"The Bronx," Rimzy replied.

It must have been the right answer, because she hit him off with two numbers to reach her. Rimzy smiled and kept it moving. As he walked out of the outlet carrying his bags, he was definitely feeling himself.

"I see nothing has changed. You still got the golden touch when it comes to the women," Black said, as they walked out the door and headed to the car.

After they passed the Tappenzee Bridge, Rimzy popped in an old school tape, and Frankie Beverly and Maze's "Before I Let Go" came oozing out of the system. At that moment, Blue pulled out an already rolled "L" of sour diesel, a high grade of marijuana.

"You wanna blow, Rimzy?" Blue asked.

Although tempted, Rimzy knew it wouldn't be a smart move.

"Nah, I got to see my Parole Officer in the morning. You know those P.O.'s stay buggin. Do you."

With that being said, Blue sparked the "L" and fogged the whip up something decent with the sweet, sticky aroma. As they got on the road home, Rimzy sat back, took a deep breath and prepared to take in the sights of a world that he could only reminisce about for seven long years. Slowly, he began to reabsorb the bliss of freedom.

The first sight to catch Rimzy's eye on the Deegan Expressway was the new Yankee Stadium. When Black zoomed across the 3rd Avenue Bridge to Manhattan and came up on 125th, Rimzy told him he wanted to get his hair braided

Black pulled up in front of the barbershop shop on 125th, and they hopped out of the whip. Rimzy was the first to enter the spot, which was somewhat crowded with people waiting for cuts and the whole nine, but Rimzy spotted a dark-skinned chocolate queen off to the side. Any other time, he wouldn't have fucked with her because he would have questioned her skills since people were waiting for other barbers, while she had no one in her chair. However, he was only getting his hair braided. If she managed to fuck that up, he would simply tell her to take it out.

Rimzy stepped straight to her and asked, "can you braid?'

Without giving a verbal response, she immediately went into a drawer in her booth and pulled out one of five photo albums she had inside. While Rimzy was going through the album, he asked Dark and Lovely her name.

"Hazel," she replied.

Rimzy picked out a simple pattern, straight braids that had a slight twist. Then, after spinning around to face Hazel, he pointed to the style. "This is what's up."

His cousins walked through the door, finagled their way off to the side, and asked him if he was straight because they had a run they had to make and would be back in about twenty minutes.

After they left, Hazel asked, "Would you like your hair washed before I braid it?"

"Yes," Rimzy replied.

After leading Rimzy to the back sink, Hazel placed a plastic cover over him and told him to lay his head back. He complied, and Hazel began to do her thing. It was like Hazel was massaging Rimzy's soul. Her hands working steadily against his scalp along with the herbal shampoo put Rimzy in a relaxed state of mind. But he wasn't too relaxed that he didn't lift his head out of the sink to see who was entering the shop every time the door opened. Time behind the wall had Rimzy on some real paranoid shit. He felt he had to be on point at all times; he didn't have any time for slip-ups.

After Hazel finished toweling Rimzy off, she finished drying his hair with a handheld dryer. She then finished lacing him up with the proper braids and held up a mirror giving him a 360 degree view of her work. Rimzy was impressed and told her so.

"I don't understand why you weren't doing anybody's hair when there are a handful of people waiting for other beauticians," he added.

"Well, I just got into this spot and haven't built up my clientele yet," Hazel explained.

"Oh okay. Well, how much do I owe you?" he asked, while reaching into his pocket.

"Thirty-five," she replied.

He handed her over fifty dollars, she thanked him, and he was out.

When he exited the shop, his cousins were waiting out front in the whip. They drove up 125th Street to Modell's and the Body Shop where Rimzy purchased a few much-needed items to maintain his appearance.

By now it was about 4:00 p.m., and Rimzy had to make a couple of stops. The first was at a little electronic store where he copped a Casio G Shock watch. Time was a valuable thing, and Rimzy had to know what time it was at all times. After he got his timepiece, they drove down to Optical Vision on 86th Street. The glasses Rimzy had on were all right for prison, but he was in the streets now and needed a better pair. Plus, he wanted to cop a pair of contact lenses.

As they entered Optical Vision, Rimzy spotted a dark-skinned honey sitting at a desk. He immediately stepped to her and asked for some assistance. When she stood up, Rimzy noticed she had on a proper burgundy Chanel business skirt and jacket, with matching stockings and Chanel shoes. Her long Indian hair pulled back accentuated her high cheekbones, giving her an exotic foreign look. The Chanel frames she had on capped off everything. She was DOING THE DAMN THANG!

When she spoke, she killed it. Rimzy never heard the words "Can I help you" sound so exotic, so intrinsically sweet. Her foreign accent was off the chart to the point where Rimzy was stuck for a second.

When he finally found the words to speak, he said, "I need an eye exam, and am interested in buying a pair of contact lenses and a pair of glasses."

"What style of glasses are you looking for?' she asked, while walking over to another counter with Rimzy and his cousins following closely behind.

Being that Rimzy was locked down for a minute, he told her he wanted a new style, preferably something thin and sleek like the ones she was wearing, but in a men's fashion. As he was talking, he surveyed the glasses inside of the glass display counter. When he laid his eyes on a pair of hot-to-death Versace glasses, he asked to see them. He put them on and they were proper, until he saw the $699 price tag attached to the arm.

"I like them, but they're not within my budget," he told the beautiful saleswoman, while handing them back to her.

She smiled. "You have nice taste. Well, about how much would you like to spend on the glasses?"

"I got about two hundred and change for a pair," he replied.

She handed him a pair of Yves Saint Laurent glasses, and Rimzy put them on. They looked good on him, and when he took them off and looked at the price, they were only $175.00. He was surprised she didn't pick out a pair closer to the limit he was willing to spend.

"There are some more expensive ones, but that pair is on sale and the best deal," she immediately told him, as if reading his mind.

At that precise moment, Rimzy couldn't hold back any longer. He had to ask this beautiful woman her name.

"Sanae," she replied in her heavenly voice.

"You have a very profound accent, Sanae. May I ask what your nationality is?"

"Eritrean," she said.

Rimzy had done a lot of intense research on Africa and knew about Eritrea and its history, and found himself fascinated with her and her culture.

After about two seconds of being stuck, Rimzy said, "Wow, Eritrea gained its independence from Ethiopia in 1993. It's a coastal region north of Ethiopia bordering the Red Sea. What is the population there?"

Now it was Sanae's turn to be stuck. No one she encountered outside of her family and native Eritreans knew the date her country gained their independence. Most people left the nationality issue alone after she told them that she was Eritrean. She knew they didn't know where it was even when they faked the impression that they did. Now, here was a nice-looking, strong, black man, not only knowing where Eritrea was, but its history as well, and also curious about other facts.

16

After about twenty seconds, in which Rimzy did not interrupt her thoughts, Sanae said, "The population is about 3.8 million."

Before she could say anything else, the eye doctor informed Rimzy that he was ready to give him the eye examination. After his test, Rimzy was told by the doctor that his glasses and contacts would be ready in a few minutes.

During that time, Rimzy conversed more with Sanae. He found out that she had been in America for ten years and that she was studying to get her Law Degree at New York Law School. She asked Rimzy how he knew about Eritrea, and he told her that he was a historian with a particular interest in esoteric sciences.

As they were talking, Rimzy paid for his purchases, and Sanae bagged them and gave him a receipt. Before they could further build on the vibe that was radiating between them, two things happened. First Sanae received a phone call, and then Blue came in the store asking Rimzy if he was almost ready because they were late and had to bounce.

Rimzy and Sanae looked at each other with unspoken words. Before turning and walking out the door, Rimzy remarked: "Have a tranquil day."

Sanae just stood in a daze and watched as he left, until her co-worker called her again about the phone.

Chapter 3

"Welcome home!" everybody yelled out in unison as soon as Rimzy walked into the dance hall the family rented for the party, and then he was rushed with hugs and kisses.

The first to reach Rimzy was his daughter, who was flanked by his youngest boy. Rimzy felt at peace being near his children, although he quickly noticed the absence of his first two boys, the twins. Rimzy could tell that this was done systematically. Everybody watched as he stooped down to get the love the children bestowed upon him. As he exchanging long awaited affections, Rimzy surveyed the crowd, particularly taking in the sights of each of their mothers. In total, Rimzy had four children—three boys and one girl—by three different women. So, believe he had plenty of baby mama drama.

First to catch his attention was Sareena, the mother of his daughter Saleena. She was on some real bullshit and perpetually kept Rimzy stressed out with any one of the many sagas that seemed to pop up every other month like clockwork. Sareena always kept a bullshit job: Pathmark, Burger King, Mickey D's type shit. That wasn't what had him stressed, though. Sareena liked fucking with lame small-time drug dealers or workers. Once, one of them smacked his daughter, and Rimzy had to send his cousins over there to spank his ass. Out of all his seeds, Saleena was the only one doing bad in school, mainly because Sareena didn't bother to see that Saleena made it to school everyday or even assist her with homework. Because Sareena failed to stress the importance of a solid education, Saleena found herself failing miserably in school. Rimzy felt himself getting angry at the whole situation and decided to look elsewhere rather than allow her bullshit to ruin the celebratory atmosphere.

Rimzy was disappointed, though not at all surprised, to see that Malika and Jewels were not in attendance. Malika called every once in a blue moon, but didn't send Rimzy's mother, who had legal custody of their seven year old son Jamal, a penny. She took some short ends from Rimzy when he got locked up, but to Rimzy this didn't warrant her ducking out of her motherly responsibilities. After all, he thought, *Malika ripping me off was between the two of us, and didn't have anything to do with Jamal.* In Rimzy's eyes, she was a selfish creep in every sense of the word. Despite it all he was still happy to see Jamal in attendance. Rimzy's thoughts then switched to the other missing piece to his puzzle.

Jewels was the mother of his first born twin sons, who were now nine years old. She was now married to a doctor and had moved to Texas. She graduated from Harvard Medical School and was an anesthesiologist. They lived in a mini mansion and were doing well. He talked to Geovani and Geovonté on the phone years ago. Rimzy was disappointed that they weren't at the party. The twins were the only children who didn't come visit him in prison. Jewels didn't even send him a picture or let him talk to them on the phone. Rimzy didn't understand how her heart could be so cold as to cut all lines of communication between himself and the twins, but he planned to straighten all of that out in due time.

Although Rimzy was overwhelmed with myriad emotions as his thoughts raced back and forth between his children and their respective mothers, Rimzy snapped out of his reminiscences and tuned back in to the matter at hand. After the children, his mother was next to get some love. Next he greeted various aunts, uncles, and cousins. Most gave him a little envelope with some paper in it. He didn't open any of them because he didn't want to seem thirsty, even though he needed all of those short ends. Rimzy noticed that each of the envelopes were the same, which led him to believe someone in the family–most likely his mother—made a speech and handed out the envelopes, on some "whatever you can spare would be greatly appreciated" shit. While Rimzy was analyzing the envelopes, Sareena approached him.

"Can I have some money to get Saleena some sneakers?" she asked.

Rimzy had to laugh. Everybody was setting him out with paper, understanding that he needed it to get on his feet, and here Sareena comes counting on his money, pressing him for a baby taste.

"Breathe easy," he told her. "I'm taking Saleena shopping later in the week."

With that said, he kept it moving. After he sorted through his paper, he was going to make sure he gave her a couple of pennies, though.

Rimzy spent the first hour with Jamal and Saleena, listening to what was on their minds and asking where they wanted to go on their first outing with their daddy. After some serious negotiating, they decided on Rye Playland.

After a lot of offers to smoke trees, which Rimzy declined, and a lot of small talk with several family members, Rimzy's cousin Rasheeda stepped to him.

"What's up, cuzzo?" she asked.

He was surprised to see how big she had gotten. When he left for jail, she was eleven years old. Now, she was eighteen and looked grown as could be. After a few minutes of reminiscing and catching up, the conversation centered on a girlfriend of hers whose father was a major drug dealer out in Maryland. She told him that he liked young girls and had just about all of them from the area. She emphasized that he didn't rape them or anything, but he was a hell of a manipulator. She explained that he had a wife and children ages seventeen, five, and one. The seventeen-year-old was her friend, and she stunted hard; so hard that she slipped up and showed her and a few other people a big safe in her basement. She said her father opened it for her one day and it was full of money.

Rimzy listened to the drama, but wasn't trying to do no juxes, especially after having only been home less than twenty-four hours. Rasheeda must have felt the vibe, because she immediately gave him an understanding nod and stated, "I know, I know. You just came home. But I still think you need to take your time and think this over." Rimzy just looked away, only half interested. Rasheeda continued "It's just that I don't trust anybody else to do the job." Still trying to gain Rimzy's trust and attention she firmly established, "if you don't do it, then it won't get done." After she said her piece, Rimzy gave her a cool and simple reply, "I'll get back to you about it." As he walked away, Rimzy replayed her proposal in his head, while considering the circumstances.

He respected how she came at him, though, especially about not trusting just anybody to do it. This showed she was a thinker. He then stashed the thought in the back of his head and got on with the celebration.

After a few more hours, the rest of the crowd began to disperse. Sareena and Saleena got a ride with one of Rimzy's uncles, so they were straight. He gave her two bills for her to walk with. Before they left, Sareena hit Rimzy with a proposition, but he refused, not wanting her to be the first one to get the dick. Nevertheless, he snatched up his baby girl, gave her a big hug, and told her that he would see her Saturday.

About this time, Black and Blue asked Rimzy if he wanted them to drop him off anywhere. He was tempted to call up his little sidekick and get his shit out of the sand, but he told himself all of that would come in time. He was going home with Mama Bear anyway, so he declined his cousins' offer.

Chapter 4

Mama Bear was Rimzy's heart. Vestra Valerie Brown was fifty-five years old and had dedicated most of her life to raising her children and grandchildren. Mama Bear had three children, all boys.

Rimzy was the middle boy. His older brother, Jackson, was killed the same year Rimzy got locked up. His younger brother, Ramel, got locked up for murdering Jackson's killer. He was currently serving twenty-five years to life up in Attica, so the family had seen its share of drama.

Mama bear lived in the same 4 bedroom apartment in the Seven Hill Project Complex for the last 25 years. She was living there with Jackson's two sons Donell and Danté, and Rimzy's son Jamal. Now with Rimzy home, each room in the house was in use. There was a point when Mama Bear was alone for almost a year, before Donell and Danté's mother dropped them off one day and never came back. Mama Bear didn't go looking for her, that was five years ago. The boys were now 8 and 9 years old.

As they pulled up in front of the building in Mama Bear's Honda Accord, Rimzy started to recall his past. He remembered playing scullies, football, baseball, and Red Light Green Light. Rimzy had many fond memories of his youth in the projects.

Rimzy's hood was tough, and his family had a reputation as being among the toughest. Rimzy's father was killed right before his 10th birthday in a drug deal gone bad. That tragic day changed Rimzy's outlook on life. It took Rimzy a year of self reflection in the Box to finally realize the vicious cycle of poverty, desperation and eventually crime that plagued his family. The hood was merely a breeding ground for toxins which had poisoned his family for too long, and Rimzy was determined to break the cycle that seemed to have engulfed his people.

When the car pulled up to the complex. Donell, Donte`and Jamal were knocked out. Rimzy woke them up so they could go inside. He figured there was no way he could carry them as well as his own bags, though somewhere in his subconscious he realized that theoretically, this was in fact what he had come home from jail to do. On Rimzy's shoulders rested the weight of each of these children, his mother, his own children and countless others, as well as his own baggage; all of which he would have to carry out of the hood, out of danger, out of the cycle in which they were trapped.

The slow ride on the elevator was hypnotic. Rimzy felt like he was caught up in a trance of familiarity, as he had ridden the same elevator so many times. When Mama Bear opened the door, the apartment looked different to Rimzy with its new furniture. His mother must have read his mind, because as they entered she mentioned that she had gotten tired of looking at the same furniture for the last 10 years. For Rimzy the small project apartment was a welcomed respite from the grey obscurity that he had just escaped.

After the children were put to bed, Rimzy and his mother reminisced for about two hours, just enjoying each other's vibe since she was off from work the next day and didn't have to worry about getting up early.

Once Mama Bear went to bed, Rimzy carried his bags into his room which Mama had so generously prepared for his return. After placing his belongings in their proper place, Rimzy took out the envelopes and started calculating the contents of all the envelopes he had accumulated. He counted eight thousand and some change, including the paper he already had upon his release. He couldn't complain. There were some people who only had the forty dollars the state gives them when they are released. "What a goddamn travesty," he thought. What do they expect a person with no family ties to do with only forty dollars and the clothes on his or her back? If Jewels hadn't sent him five G's, his net worth would have been drastically reduced. So, he was very thankful. He definitely had to make it his business to get out there and see the twins, but he knew he had to come to correct.

More thoughts flooded his mind as Rimzy took off his undergarments, ripped open a fresh bar of Yardley's soap, and went to take a nice, long, hot shower. It had been a minute since he had that luxury, because while incarcerated, they were only given five minutes to shower. Being that his zodiac sign was Pisces, he often felt like he was one with the water, and being rushed while showering had a way of throwing Rimzy out of synch. Old habits were hard to break, because as he was in the shower, he started planning for the next day. The first thing he had to do was go see his parole officer. After that, he had to go shopping. But first things first, he was going to cook Mama Bear and the children a nice breakfast.

After showering, he walked over to the mirror, posed for a minute, smiled, and yelled, "FREEDOM!"

Chapter 5

Six hours of sleep was all it took for Rimzy to feel completely rejuvenated. It seemed like all the while he was in a semi state of consciousness. He guessed the anxiety of finally being home wouldn't let his mind shut down completely. He found that to be strange, because it was the same way in prison. He would never allow himself to regress into that comfortable state called sleep.

After washing his face, brushing his teeth, and throwing on a pair of sweatpants, a tank top, socks, and slippers, he made his way to the kitchen. It was a small kitchen, but it was immaculately clean. A lot of love was spread in that there kitchen.

Rimzy opened the refrigerator and wasn't surprised to see it filled with all kinds of food He decided to make some home fries, beef sausage and turkey bacon, along with banana pancakes. Once Rimzy had everything he needed he began mixing slicing and dicing. It felt a little funny cutting with a knife since he had grown use to cutting everything with can tops for the past seven years. At that moment, the subtle reality of his new freedom set in and Rimzy savored it. He continued cooking in the hopes that he could capture the same sweet taste in his food in order to convey this happiness to his loved ones.

After everything was done, he placed the food on the table and went to wake up the children, telling them to brush their teeth and wash up. While they were doing that, he prepared a tray consisting of banana pancakes, home fries, bacon, sausage, herbal tea, and orange juice, and took it to his mother's room.

"Come in," Mama Bear called out sleepily when he knocked on her bedroom door.

When he entered, he noticed the look of surprise on his mother's face. "I don't know what you're looking surprised about," he told her. "A queen gets what her hand calls for, which is the best."

With that being said, he placed the tray over her lap and eased out the room to let her enjoy her meal.

* * * * * *

When Blue pulled up to take Rimzy to go see his P.O., Rimzy was outside the building waiting. The trip to 161st wasn't too long. They were double-parked in front of an impressive building with a large plaque displaying the corresponding floor and suite numbers for the Parole, Welfare and SSI offices. Rimzy scoped out his destination then turned to Blue, who would stay in the car while he went inside to take care of his business, and gave him a pound.

After entering the building, Rimzy took the elevator to the 9th floor where there was a large waiting area with a desk. He went to the front and asked to see Parole Officer Davis. It was 9:05 a.m. and crowded as hell. After about forty minutes, he was finally called and directed toward the third room on the right.

As he entered the office, he came face to face with a fat, white male, who told Rimzy to sit down and then hit him with the orientation speech, explaining who he was and what he expected of Rimzy. He told Rimzy that he would be conducting random urinalysis tests and was issuing him a nine o'clock curfew. In addition, he expected Rimzy to seek and maintain employment as soon as possible. After about twenty minutes of the dos and don'ts of his parole, Rimzy was out of there.

When Rimzy got outside, he jumped in the whip and they hit the Deegan up to Westchester. Rimzy was headed to go see Shabazz, his man who had a construction coalition. When they got there, Shabazz set him up with a two year job on a high rise in mid town paying 20 dollars an hour. Rimzy was happy with the job and thanked his man for the hook up. He gave Rimzy a hard hat, some gloves and told him he could start in 2 days.

From there, Rimzy and his cousin jetted over to Westbury Outlets. When it was all said and done, Rimzy had spent about three G's, purchasing about twenty outfits, from sweat suits to slacks. He also copped a black suit just in case, God forbid, he had to go to a funeral. On the footwear check, he purchased four pairs of sneakers, four more pairs of boots, and two pairs of dress shoes. Basically, he was set. He ran into a lot of good deals. If he would have shopped in the city, he would've probably gotten half of the things he got from the outlets. By the time they drove off, Rimzy had accumulated fifteen bags worth of fashions. He copped Blue a couple of outfits, too. He was definitely flooded out on the wears check.

When they reached the P.J.'s Rimzy looked at his watch and saw that it was 3:00 p.m. Wanting to straighten out his license at the DMV before it closed, they ran all of the bags upstairs, set them down, and headed right back out the door. Essentially, all Rimzy had to do was take and submit a more recent picture in order to have a new license sent to him; he had already renewed it while in jail. It seemed like an easy task, but they didn't walk out of the motor vehicle center until 5:45 p.m.

After the bullshit at the DMV, Blue dropped Rimzy off at his mother's and kept it moving. As soon as Rimzy got off the elevators, he smelled the food bubbling and knew it was coming from Apartment 7-D. When he opened the door, Mama Bear was putting that supreme love on the food. Rimzy gave his mother a kiss and asked if the food was almost ready. Mama told him that the food would be ready in ten minutes. Rimzy smiled in response and moved down the hall where Jamal, Danté and Donell were in their room playing Playstation. Rimzy stepped into the room and hugged his son and nephews. "What's poppin," he added.

"Nothing," they replied in unison.

Rimzy was tempted to grab them and mess up their game, but he decided against it. Instead, he kept it moving to his room, where he occupied his free time by packing away all of his new purchases and organizing what few possessions he had. Rimzy was so accustomed with keeping his small cell block space organized that it felt natural to him even on the outside. He already finished, and was first emerging from a quick shower when Mama Bear called out that dinner was ready. Rimzy changed into one of his new outfits and glided out of the room, feeling good. Everything he had on was new; no more state greens. *Yes*, he thought, *today is a good day.*

Everyone was at the table eating when Rimzy sat down to a plate of baked macaroni and cheese, peas & rice, and southern fried chicken. *Things never change,* he thought. Even when he was young, Rimzy knew when to get his ass upstairs to eat. The next generation just followed the tradition. It was truly a *New York State of Mind.*

Chapter 6

Rimzy had met a few women since he came home, but the one in the glasses store stood out by far. He went to the glasses store a couple of times, but she was never there. Rimzy had almost given up on her, but one day he broke his glasses while working on a construction site and needed another pair.

It was raining hard when Rimzy pulled up in front of the eyeglass store. It seemed as though the sky had opened up and released a long, built-up fury that needed to be let loose. Rimzy stepped into the store wearing an official fatigue rain suit, with a hood and a pair of green ACG boots on his feet. He stomped hard two or three times to relieve the excess water on him, and then proceeded to walk to the counter.

"Is Sanae working?"

The clerk gave him a once over, then told him that she was in the back. He asked the clerk to tell Sanae that a big customer of hers would like her to personally assist him with his order.

"No problem, sir," the clerk said, as he spun off to deliver the message. Two minutes later, Sanae came out. When Rimzy entered the store the first time, he thought he was just thirsty, which is why Sanae looked so good. She walked toward him in a little white dress with a pink belt around her small waist, matching pink sandals and Prada sunglasses perched on her head which was coiffed with a neat ponytail. He was instantly reassured that his initial impression of her radiant looks wasn't just because he was released that day. Once again she had a natural glow that made her shine like a star.

"Hello, Sanae. It's a beautiful thing seeing you today. I broke my glasses and was hoping you could replace them". She smiled and responded, "That shouldn't be a problem. I heard you came in a while back and asked for me."

"Most definitely. I heard you were studying hard for your finals. They should be over now, so what topic did you write your thesis on?"

Sanae didn't know what it was about this man that made him always have the right questions. Her fiancé, whom her parents seemed to be more interested in than her, made it obvious that he wasn't interested in her studies. Sanae zoned out for a couple of seconds and returned to reality with a smiling Rimzy looking at her.

"I wrote it on the symbolism of the ancient crown in Egypt."

"Wow, that's a deep subject. Did you go into the science of the pineal gland?"

Sanae was taken aback. "Yes, I touched on the Black Dot, but there is so little information on the subject. I couldn't go into it like I wanted."

"I wish I would have known earlier. I could've referred you to a book by Dr. Richard King called *The African Origin of Biological Psychiatry*."

As he went into detail about the science of the Black Dot, Sanae took out her Blackberry and transcribed the name of the book and the author's name.

"I really wanted to see you again." Rimzy looked into her eyes, but there was no indication she felt the same way. "Basically, what I'm trying to say is that I enjoy talking to you and would love to get to know you better. Being that you've just gotten your Masters, I think congratulations and a celebration are in order. I just happen to have two tickets to see Mary J. Blige in two days, and I was hoping you would allow me the honor of taking you out to dinner and to see her in concert."

Sanae was speechless. She was attracted to Rimzy, but had just gotten herself out of a very bad four-year relationship. She didn't know if she was ready to complicate her life again. Well, actually she broke up with her fiancé seven months prior, and she told herself that she didn't need any men in her life. She needed to put all of her energy into school.

On the other hand, she had finished school a month ago and deserved to treat herself to a night out on the town. Besides, she wanted to see Mary. *It's not like we're getting married*, she reasoned to herself internally, *it's just a date.*

She snapped out of her zone after convincing herself that she would go. She realized she must have been in thought for about three minutes. What was impressive about Rimzy is he didn't interrupt her. Any other man would have rushed her for an answer. Instead, Rimzy just stood there, smiling and patiently waiting for her answer.

"Normally, I don't do this." She handed Rimzy her card with her phone number. "I don't even know you, but you're right. I do need to get out, if only for one night."

Being as sharp as he was, Rimzy read between the lines. Basically, she was letting him know not to get his hopes up. More than likely, this was going to be the first and last date.

Timing is the key for all major moves in life, Rimzy thought. He knew if he would've pressed Sanae at another point in time, she would've turned him down flat.

"Now that the personal stuff is out the way, let's get down to business. Which are the hottest specs on the planet right now?"

Rimzy left the store with a pair of Yves Saint Laurent glasses, and—the most important thing of all—a date with Sanae.

After walking to the door, he grabbed the handle and spun around quickly to meet Sanae's intense gaze. They both waved goodbye one more time before Rimzy dashed outside, into the rain.

Chapter 7

Two days later, Rimzy pulled in front of Sanae's apartment building in Blue's Maxima, which he borrowed for the night. Sanae came out wearing a breezy white summer dress with a pair of Tory Burch wedge sandals. Her jewelry brought out her outfit. She had on a seashell choker with the matching ankle and wrist bracelets. She had her hair braided in an exotic pattern that came down over the shoulders, giving her a look reminiscent of the great Nefertiti.

Rimzy stepped outside to open the door for her and without breaking her stride, she slid right in. As soon as he reentered the car, Rimzy was assaulted with an exotic, all-natural mixture of raspberries and vanilla. Their eyes were smiling when they connected.

"I don't know how you do it, but you seem to look better and better every time I see you," Rimzy complimented. "I love your hairstyle. It brings out the definition in your cheekbones."

Sanae blushed. Her mother had also told her that when she pushed her hair back it accentuated her cheekbones. She thought to herself, *what is it with this man that always makes him say the right things?*

"We're a little early for the show, so would you like to get something to eat?" Rimzy asked her, changing the subject.

"Sure, sounds good."

It took Rimzy no time to maneuver to a nice Caribbean restaurant called Negril on W. 3rd Street. They found a parking lot one block away. As they were walking to Negril, Rimzy realized he dominated the conversation on the drive. He resolved within himself to let Sanae open up over dinner because he wanted to learn much more about her.

Once inside, they were ushered to a cozy table for two, which was located off to the side with a view of busy W. 3rd Street. A few seconds later, a waiter appeared and disposed of two menus without saying a word. When the waiter reappeared, Rimzy ordered the crab patty appetizer, and for his main entrée, he ordered the oxtail served over coconut rice. He also ordered a rum punch. Sanae ordered steamed king fish over coconut rice, with steamed broccoli. Her drink of choice was chardonnay.

After the waiter left with the order, Rimzy asked Sanae, "Chardonnay is your drink of choice, or are you taking it easy tonight?"

"I guess a little of both. Overall, I'm a very moderate drinker."

"It's funny you say that because I consider myself a moderate drinker, also. Listen, I'm going to keep it official. I smoke marijuana. I hope you don't think any less of me for addressing my vices with you."

Sanae didn't like the fact that Rimzy smoked, but it was something she could deal with. Her father smoked for as long as she could remember and he was her idol.

"I respect your honesty. I guess everybody is entitled to their own vices."

Rimzy, not missing a beat, changed the subject. "So tell me, was it a hard adjustment coming to this country?"

"I'm very fortunate that my family is financially stable. I've never been in a financial struggle, so I've been able to concentrate a lot of my energy toward my education. Basically, I'm a homebody. I don't really go out much. I'm far from a party girl. I don't have a lot of friends. Not to sound conceited, but most people I meet wind up disappointing me with ignorant things that come out of their mouths or their ways and actions. I'm not saying that because I have my masters. I've met people who have their masters and are still ignorant to the finer things in life."

As if on cue, the waiter came with their food. Rimzy was feeling Sanae's vibe. She was giving it up raw and uncut. While they were eating dinner Rimzy found out that Sanae was trying to use her undergraduate degree in sociology to open up a nonprofit organization specializing in troubled youth. She was in the midst of formulating her proposal to obtain some federal grants. She hoped to get everything off the ground by the time she finished her Law degree. Rimzy was very impressed.

After they ate, the waiter came over. "Is everything satisfactory?" he asked, then said, "If I may suggest a piece of banana walnut cake. It just came out of the oven, and it goes simply marvelous with the vanilla hazelnut cappuccino."

Rimzy noticed when the waiter said marvelous, he put a little extra in it, insinuating that he was gay. Rimzy didn't have a problem with gay people...to each his or her own. As long as they respected his boundaries, everything was all good. They took the waiter up on his suggestion and weren't at all disappointed. Both Rimzy and Sanae appreciated good food.

Rimzy consulted his watch to find out they were in the restaurant for almost two hours. The time went by so fast. That was a good thing because if it would have seemed like four hours, that would've meant time was dragging and Sanae's conversation wasn't captivating. After catching the waiter's attention, Rimzy signaled for the check. The waiter acknowledged Rimzy with a slight nod of his head and brought over the check. Rimzy paid the waiter in cash and thanked him for his immaculate service with a decent tip.

While waiting in the parking lot for the attendant to bring his car, Rimzy couldn't help realizing how happy he felt in Sanae's company. When the car pulled up, he immediately opened the door for Sanae and closed it softly after she was in.

Once inside, Rimzy hit a few buttons and Jill Scott's "My Way" came oozing out of the stereo system. They drove down 6th Avenue until they got to 43rd Street, where they found a park right before the corner of Broadway. Usually, Rimzy parked his whips in parking lots because he would rather pay shorts at the lot versus coming out and finding his car broken into. However, Broadway was a very busy street, so Rimzy took a chance.

It was a very short walk to BB King's on 42nd Street. Once inside, they were ushered over to a cozy table for two in front of the stage. Before their first drinks were finished, Mary came out and bombarded them with a string of hits. Rimzy didn't know if it was the smooth grooves of Mary, the drinks, or Sanae giving him a sense of euphoria. In any event, he was riding high on a wave and was not trying to come down.

After the show, they strolled down Broadway. Rimzy glanced at his watch, which read 12:45 a.m.

"I know it's getting kind of late, but I know this nice pool hall down on 21st Street and…"

Before Rimzy could finish his uncomfortable sentence, Sanae said, "I would like that."

Rimzy just smiled. He was really feeling Sanae.

When they entered the pool hall, Rimzy rented a table for an hour. Sanae ordered a fruit punch drink, while Rimzy decided on having a Corona. Rimzy noticed Sanae must have felt a little more comfortable because she stopped drinking chardonnay. Rimzy was surprised to see that Sanae was a pool shark. She had mad game. At first, she was acting all innocent like she didn't know how to play.

Rimzy was in his glory showing Sanae the fundamentals of the game. He showed her a couple of pointers, like hitting the cue ball low so it would spin backward and not scratch on an easy shot. Rimzy was lying low, watching Sanae's bubble as she bent over to make certain shots. He was tempted to go up behind her and help her with her form, but decided against that particular move.

Sanae flipped the tables on him the next game by saying, "Let's make this game interesting by making a friendly wager."

Rimzy was against her idea because he thought he was a better pool player than Sanae and felt it would be taking advantage of her. Sanae kept insisting until Rimzy finally broke down and agreed. He figured he could take it easy on her. Come to find out, Rimzy only got one shot the whole game. She was sinking three cushion bank shots and the whole nine. At the end, all Rimzy could do was smile. He thought he was going to take it easy on her, but in all actuality, she took it easy on him.

"Let me find out," Rimzy said, while reaching into his pocket.

Sanae stopped his movement by placing her hand over his, which was now in his pocket. "Hold on to your money. I was just joking with you. My father kept a pool table in our house as long as I could remember, and I just took to it. I used to compete, but it required too much traveling."

Rolling with the flow, Rimzy asked her to show him a couple of trick shots. They wound up getting the table for another hour and Rimzy learned enough moves to become an amateur pool shark. That night, he stepped up his pool game five notches. Now it was Sanae's turn to smile. She tried the same trick on her ex-fiancé, but he got on some male ego shit and just wound up frustrating himself. Sanae was definitely feeling Rimzy's vibe.

On the way back to her place, Rimzy put on Rome's first CD and they rode the melodious waves uptown in silence, each in their own thoughts.

As they pulled up in front of Sanae's building, Rimzy said, "I really had a beautiful time in your company. I don't know what it is about you, but you are a breath of fresh air in this stale environment. I'm hoping you'll give us the opportunity to get to know each other much better."

Sanae felt like saying she felt the same way, but decided to be reserved. "I would like that."

Rimzy reached over and they kissed. No tongue, just a meeting of the lips. When their lips disconnected, he gave her bottom lip another small peck. On that note, Sanae opened the door and stepped outside.

As a second thought, she leaned back in the car and said, "I really enjoyed tonight."

Then she spun around and walked to her building a few feet away. Rimzy watched with a smile, as they both made eye contact for the last time before her retreating figure left his view.

Damn, she was one sexy, intriguing, intelligent woman.

Chapter 8

Rimzy posted up in front of his Mother's building with a cool demeanor that was in large contrast to the anticipatory flood of thoughts rushing through his head. As he waited in silence, he thought long and hard about the special lady whom he awaited. He thought about how he respected her because she made it clear she was doing big things with her life independently. He liked that about her.

His thought process was interrupted as a sleek Acura pulled up in front of him. Rimzy took a good look and confirmed to himself that Sanae was inside. She picked a spot on the curb, put the car in park and switched off the ignition; Rimzy took in each movement she made, relishing in his newly regained ability to observe such a fine specimen freely in their natural environment. Sanae got out and looked around for him. She had on an Anne Klein charcoal gray "knock 'em dead" business skirt, white blouse, and a gray blazer, with grey pumps. Once she met his gaze, she began to make her way across the sidewalk to the spot where he had perched. They approached each other with smiles, their bodies embraced and their lips met. After their embrace they started walking toward her car. Once inside, she started the ignition and the smooth sounds of Mary J. Blige's "Your Child" filled the interior bringing back sweet memories of their first date.

Sanae drove down Castle Hill Avenue until she hit Randel, then she made a left until she reached White Plains Road. From there, it was off to the Cross Bronx Expressway to the Major Deagan

Expressway. By the time Mary's CD was coming to its end, Sanae was pulling in the underground parking lot of Tracy Towers.

Sanae lived on the 34th floor of the building which went up to forty-two stories. As Rimzy entered the apartment for the first time, he wasn't surprised at the fine décor. Sanae had the proper beige carpet with specks of brown which coordinated just right with the milky off-white matching sofa, love seat, and recliner. One wall had a cream unit with an impressive entertainment system equipped with a 52-inch Sony Bravia TV. The other two walls had floor-to-ceiling mirrors that gave the room a bedazzling effect. Rimzy was definitely feeling Sanae's lab.

When Sanae picked up the remote control and hit a button, all kind of lights illuminated the entertainment system. Then the smooth sounds of R. Kelly's "Don't Put Me Out" vibrated from all corners of the room's surround sound. The music was low, but it had crazy bass, just the way Rimzy liked it.

After about thirty minutes of zoning, Sanae came sashaying down the hallway toward the living room. She had on a black, thin satin robe, which was drawn tight at the waist, with a pair of sheer black fishnet stockings peeking from underneath and a pair of black 6-inch pumps. Her long black hair with those almond shaped eyes put her over the top.

When she reached Rimzy, she leaned over provocatively, kissed him on the cheek, and licked her way down to his neck, before sucking on it for about three seconds.

Soon after, she sat down, looked at the 'L' and the bubbly, and asked, "Why didn't you pop that?"

"I was waiting on you so we can make a toast and enjoy the session together."

She smiled and kissed him again on the neck. By now, Rimzy was open. Sanae smelled like vanilla and almonds. He was ready to skip everything else and just start digging her back out, but one thing Rimzy learned in prison was patience, especially considering the fact that this was their first time being intimate. So, he just relaxed, enjoyed the moment, and proceeded to pop the Moet. After pouring two glasses, he made a toast.

"To life and everything beautiful in it."

They clanked their glasses together and drank. When Rimzy put his drink down, he picked up the 'L' and fired it up. At once, the pungent odor filled the air.

After a few pulls, he passed it to Sanae, who surprisingly knew exactly what to do. She pulled it to her lips and drew a dainty breath, returning it to Rimzy as she exhaled. Once the "L" was finished and a couple glasses of bubbly were absorbed, it seemed like they reached a higher state of existence. Rimzy was the truth, and sometimes when he reached a higher plane, he liked to get his build on. This was one of those times.

One of the things that attracted Rimzy to Sanae was her ability to vibe with him on an intellectual level. Rimzy had experienced a fair share of women in his lifetime; he was no longer driven unilaterally by the flesh. It took much more than that to turn him on. He looked at Sanae in her splendor and smiled. "You are doing well, I see," he remarked "you look good, nice crib, nice car, body right." She returned his smile and responded "Yea, but at this moment, all of that is irrelevant. All that matters is me and you, here, together. With that alone I am content." Rimzy was completely captivated. This is why he adored Sanae. When it came down to it, she was of the same state of mind as Rimzy. He took hold of the opportunity to converse. "Sanae, the plight of a lot of people is that they're bound up in the world of illusion and ignorance, thinking it is real, unaware of their true identification," he started.

"Tell me more," Sanae purred, wholly interested in the topic at hand. This turned Rimzy on both mentally and physically. They were both engaged in this mind sex. Rimzy continued, "A perfect example of what I'm talking about is the parable of the tiger that was orphaned as a cub and reared by goats. All of his life he actually believed he was a goat. He ate grass and the whole nine. One day, he met another tiger who took him to a pond where he saw his true image. After this, the other tiger forced him to eat meat. For the first time, he slowly began to realize his true tiger nature." Sanae listened intently and shook her head for Rimzy to go on.

"In the same manner, people are deceived about their true nature; it is up to a person to elevate themselves and learn to live on their new plane. Right now, I'm trying to reach my highest self which is eternally pure, intelligent, and free! My entire complex of phenomenal existence is striving for perfection. As I strive forward, my analysis becomes sharper, the challenges more radical, and the commitment open and precise." As Sanae listened she realized the extent to which Rimzy's experiences has molded him in to the driven man that sat before her. She was enamored with his realized drive. She thought to herself, *I want him.* Rimzy took another pull on his L and exhaled, intoxicating them both with the herb and his words.

He continued, "A lot of people worship ignorance, which causes them to enter blinding darkness or have tunnel vision. Their main focus is material items. Look at the American Dream: house, car, and money in the bank. There is more to life than mere material items, but it is the norm of this society. What happened to family, companionship, peace, love, and happiness…The Universal Laws of Life?"

Sanae felt herself moving closer to him. She wanted to show him all of these things. As he bought the 'L' in again, she took the opportunity to let him know this.

"I want to meet you on that elevated plane Rimzy. All of this around us is material. But what we have seems spiritual and unique." Rimzy felt her statement. "Don't get me wrong, love. This is a materialistic world, and there is nothing wrong with wanting the best material items. I'm not going to front. I want the best, but I want the best on every plane. You see, a lot of people have a reductionist style of thinking that simplifies life into just material items and nothing else...when that is just the basics. There is so much more to life. I know my history and I know our ancestors were kings and queens. So, it is only right that I follow the tradition of my ancestors and live like a king and have my queen at my side."

As Rimzy came out of his zone, he looked over at Sanae and saw that she was hanging on his every word and not lost. Rimzy despised an ignorant woman and Sanae, for sure, was not that.

When Sanae caught Rimzy trying to look in between the folds of her robe, she gave him a kiss, stood up, and let the robe drop to the floor. She had on a black lacey g-string and matching bra. Her stockings stopped mid-thigh, revealing her beautiful black skin. She turned around and touched her toes, allowing her hot box to poke through the back. When she stood up, she arched her back so her butt looked perfect. She put on a little show for Rimzy, slow dancing, putting one foot on the table, and gyrating. She was definitely in her glory. While she was performing, Rimzy was slowly taking his clothes off. After her little performance, she positioned herself between Rimzy's legs and started kissing his neck. He was butt-ass naked by this time.

Sanae went from his neck to his chest, then sunk her knees into the soft textured carpet and started planting hot, passionate kisses up and down the length of Rimzy's soul bone. In between kisses, she would lick him from his scrotum all the way to the head of his shaft. She knew the effect she was having on Rimzy, but refused to give it to him the way she knew he wanted it. After a few minutes of teasing, she started licking fast right under his head, then formed an "O" with her mouth and began to suck him, moving her head up and down, swallowing up half his dick. Soon, the back muscles in her throat started to open up and she removed her hand from the base of his shaft, except for her thumb and forefinger, and started deep-throating him.

Rimzy was amazed because no woman had ever been able to get the whole nine inches of his manhood down her throat. Sanae started switching gears, applying maximum suction like a vacuum cleaner. This took Rimzy over the top. When he started fighting on the sofa, she knew he was going to bust off, but she kept on, concentrating on the head. When he let off, he expected her to stop, but she swallowed every drop. After she milked him, she kept on sucking, making sure he was done. When she finished, she grabbed Rimzy's hand and led him to the bedroom. Once there, she told him to hold on a minute while she went to brush her teeth and gargle with some mouthwash.

When Sanae entered the bedroom, Rimzy was waiting on the bed. Suddenly, they were in each other's arms, their lips locked. Rimzy sucked urgently at Sanae's voluptuous lips, sending a shiver vibrating all the way down to the insides of her thighs. He worked his lips down to her breast and started sucking her big, round, brown nipples. Sanae had proper grapefruit size titties, and Rimzy loved every minute of them. While sucking on one breast, he rubbed the other.

Soon, he worked one of his hands down under her g-string to test the waters. A finger swished through the wet slickness of her love box. When Rimzy stuck his middle finger inside of her, she let out a sigh and opened her legs wider. Rimzy could tell by her heavy breathing that she was more than ready for him to put in work. Sanae started arching her back, trying to get as much of Rimzy's finger as she could.

At this point, Rimzy pulled his finger out with a popping sound he made his way down to her succulent thighs and started massaging them with his lips and tongue. Soon he made his way up to her love box. When he arrived, he was like a kid in a candy store, eating away. Between the licking, sucking and nibbling, Sanae was in a frenzy. Rimzy slowly worked his way up to mount her. First, he put the head of his penis around her opening and started rubbing it against her. Sanae started lifting her ass off of the bed, trying to get the bonus.

"Come on, baby," she begged. "Give it to me now."

"You sure?"

"Yes, yes, yes."

After the third yes, Rimzy entered her hot, tight insides, sliding easily through her quivering cunt lips. Her pussy was slick, but still a tight fit for Rimzy's width. He had to put a little corkscrew motion on his Johnson to make it slide in gracefully.

Sanae tried to hold a steady rhythm, rotating her ass in time to match Rimzy's love strokes, but it was hard to keep from going crazy. The entire inner lining of her pussy tingled from the glorious contact of his expertly controlled fuck bone.

After about ten minutes of this position, Sanae threw her head back and started shaking while calling out Rimzy's name. She expected Rimzy to bust off because the contractions in her pussy crashed down on his dick with a fury, but Rimzy didn't miss a beat. He rode her through waves of ecstasy as she dug her nails in his back. Rimzy had her legs on his shoulders and watched as her toes curled and released in climax. Slowly, Sanae came down from the orgasms that didn't want to quit. She lay limp for a time, too drained to attempt to move, while Rimzy pumped away.

Suddenly, Rimzy pulled out, flipped Sanae over on all fours, and entered her doggy style. After a few strokes, Sanae started pushing her fat ass backwards, banging against Rimzy's belly. The smacking noises their bodies made were erotic, and before Sanae knew it, her elbows sagged, causing her belly to sink to the bed as another orgasm came vibrantly alive. She was tensing and shuddering, not only deep inside her womb, but throughout her entire body. She was screaming in ecstasy.

Her earth-shattering contractions brought Rimzy over the top. He jerked, then lunged and held himself to the deepest point as his long delayed ejaculations sent specs of hot liquid into her inner depths. Rimzy felt like his balls were going to explode as his muscles flexed to release heated spurts of love juice.

Chapter 9

Rimzy walked toward Mama's building in a fog of pleasant memories. He thought about the intensity of his affection for Sanae and reminisced about their time together. They had become so close and were spending more and more time together since their first intimate encounter. He thought about how well things were going in his broader life. Two months had passed and everything was going good for Rimzy. They were working him like a mule at his job, but Rimzy didn't mind. He was happy to be working making decent money, plus he had a lot of stamina and endurance due to the intense weight lifting he endured everyday in prison.

His foreman recognized that Rimzy was a hard worker and blessed him with overtime almost every day. Since he didn't have any major bills, he was saving most of his money. It was a slow hard grind and he wasn't used to that, but at least he didn't have to look over his shoulder for the cops or stick up kids. He appreciated working and getting a check every week. He figured that he should have enough money to go see the twins in a few more weeks. Rimzy's curfew kept him from doing too much.

He had to be in by 9PM and by the time he got home from all the overtime he was getting it was a wrap. On the weekends he spent most of his time with the children. He felt good reestablishing meaningful relationships with the family, especially Mama Bear and the kids.

Things were going excellent between Rimzy and Sanae. Because of his curfew, Sanae spent more than her share of nights in Mama Bear's apartment. Mama Bear and the kids loved Sanae.

There were four fire trucks in front of Mama Bear's building when he got out of the Dollar Cab coming from work. His senses were a little dull after being in prison for all of those years. He was on point, but he saw a lot of things during his incarceration. For instance, he could see somebody get stabbed in the eye right in front of him and just keep it moving like it wasn't anything. The last thing he thought was that it was his mother's apartment the fire trucks were there for. There were so many apartments in his mother's building that the odds were slim that it was hers.

All of that changed when he scanned the crowd and saw both of his nephews crying. At that point, he dropped his construction hat and started running.

"Is everybody alright?" he asked when he reached his nephews.

"Yes," responded his nephew.

"What happened?"

In between all of the sniffling, Rimzy learned that Donell had tried to make some French fries and burned the apartment down. The firemen were coming out of the building as they were talking.

Rimzy told the boys to stay there while he went upstairs to check on things. Once he weaved his way through the noisy emergency workers in the hallway, he finally got to the apartment to find his mother and a couple of her friends.

He and his mother made eye contact, then ran and hugged each other. He told her not to worry herself about things. As long as everybody was safe, that is all that mattered. After a quick surveillance, Rimzy came to the conclusion that everything in the apartment was lost...pictures, clothing, furniture, everything.

After a few phone calls, the children were relocated. Rimzy's incarcerated brother Ramel's wife Butter took the boys. She was a sweetheart. Black's girlfriend Coco took in Mama Bear.

When Rimzy called Sanae to tell her about the fire, she offered her condolences and told him he could stay with her. Rimzy felt she didn't deserve to have to deal with this, but under the circumstances, he felt it would be best if he stayed with her temporarily until he got on his feet. By the time Rimzy got to Sanae's lab, he felt sick and tired of being sick and tired. They discussed the day's happenings and Rimzy tried to figure out a plan. He was bent. Not only did he need a wardrobe, but so did his mother and nephews. Thank goodness he opened a bank account and three stacks on the books; the rest of his money went up in smoke in a shoe box.

The next day, Rimzy went to work with a lot on his mind. During lunch, he stopped at the bank and withdrew two stacks to give to his mother so she could get her and the children some new clothes. He told her that he should have another thousand for her the next day. Even though Sanae told him she would have two G's for him when she came home from work, he was waiting for it to be in his hands before he gave up his last bit of paper. He couldn't afford to give away all his money in the event that Sanae couldn't come through for him.

Enough is enough. Things were out of control the next couple of weeks for Rimzy. The home court drama wasn't the only thing that had him bent. He had recently spoke with his brother, who was currently serving a 25-year-to-life sentence for killing their older brother's killer and his man, who told him that he met this kid who had a lawyer that had mad pull in the Bronx Supreme Court.

He said he spoke to the lawyer on a three-way call, and the lawyer told him if he paid him two G's, he would look at his paperwork and see if he could get him either a reversal or some type of time served plea deal. The price tag for his brother's freedom was $125,000. That is, if the lawyer could finagle something that could grant him freedom.

To top it all off, he couldn't take his children out the way he wanted to, and he still didn't get down to Texas to see the twins.

What really put him over the top was when he went to go see his mother at his cousin's house. His mother was on the phone and Co-Co, in a semi-hostile tone, told Mama Bear that she would have to call back whoever she was talking to because she had to make a call. Mama Bear hung up, but when she spun around, she had a look in her eye that almost made Rimzy cry. She looked defeated.

It was at that precise moment all of the staying focused shit he learned to apply to his life while in prison went out the window. He couldn't tolerate any chicken-head, goose-neck chick dictating anything to his moms. Shit, she was a dictator; she was his queen.

On that note, he gave Mama Bear two thousand dollars and told her, "I got to go take care of something, so stay sweet and stay strong. Everything is going to work itself out real soon. Love ya."

After leaving, Rimzy made a call to his cousin. "I need to see you as soon as possible about that thing we talked about," he said after she picked up.

"I'm coming to town this weekend," she responded, and then they hung up.

His next call was to Blue, "What it do player. We need to talk face to face about some serious shit."

Chapter 10

There wasn't too much to talk about on the road. Rimzy and Blue were as sober as could be. Rimzy made sure of this. Bad enough they were jumping out the window. They had to be one hundred percent focused on their landing or it was a wrap. Everything was on the line; there was no second chance. Each of them was deep within their self, but more or less thinking the same thoughts.

When they pulled into the Mickey Ds parking lot, they were five minutes early, so Blue went to get some food. While he was inside, baby girl pulled alongside of their vehicle just as she was instructed. They both opened their doors and the transaction was made. She then went inside to get some food.

When Blue got back in the truck, Rimzy pulled off. Immediately, Blue put the food down and started getting into his disguise. Once he finished putting on his makeup, he looked at Rimzy, who gave him the okay that all was good.

After stopping at the next stop sign, Blue jumped in the driver's seat while Rimzy put on his Federal Express uniform. Three minutes later, Rimzy was walking up the front steps of Mr. Durell's driveway with a long box in one hand and a clipboard, pen, and scanner in the other.

While Rimzy was on his way to the door, Blue drove five blocks away to a 24-hour Wal-Mart parking lot. He parked off to the side with the back of the van against a fence and some bushes. Once he stopped, he looked around, went to the front of the van, and removed the front New Jersey license plate.

Meanwhile, back at the house, Rimzy rang the bell and a pleasant lady came to the door. She opened the door, but there was still a big heavy-duty screen door between them. As she stood there,

Rimzy put on the country accent that he and Rasheeda had practiced every day until he had that country drawl down pat.

She looked puzzled, as if she wasn't expecting a delivery, until Rimzy explained it was a special rush delivery from Aunt B's Flower Boutique. Mrs. Durell figured her husband sent her flowers and was eager to see them. So, when Rimzy shifted the box like it was falling, then clumsily motioned for her to sign the clipboard he was holding with the pen that was slipping out of his hand, she thought nothing of opening the screen door. It wasn't until she lifted her eyes from signing the clipboard and she saw the big shiny desert eagle pointed at her chest did she realized why her husband told her to never open the screen door to strangers.

"Don't say a word," Rimzy told her.

It was then that she realized there was no Federal Express van parked in front of her house. By the time she snapped out of her zone, Rimzy was already in the house. With her hands behind her back, he handcuffed her to the banister pole of the stairs.

He then told her in a quiet, yet stern voice, "This is only a robbery. Everything will work out okay if you do as I say and do not lie to me. If you cause me any complications, I will kill you and everyone in this house. Do you understand me?"

"Yes," she responded with a quivering voice.

"How many people are in the house?"

"Just me and my two children."

"Where are they?"

"Upstairs."

"What are they doing?"

"Sleeping," she replied.

"Open your mouth," he told her, and when she did, he shoved a sock in it and tied a knot in the back of her head with a folded bandana. He then put another one over her eyes. "Now stay completely still."

He then checked every room and closet on the first level. Next, he went upstairs and checked every room. The children were sleeping like she said.

Before he went back downstairs, he coughed two times into a mini walkie-talkie, which was the signal to let Blue know it was all good and for him to start his way back to him.

When he reached the bottom of the stairs, he took the sock out of Mrs. Durell's mouth. "I don't want to hurt you. All I want is the money. Now I'm going to ask you a question and your life depends on your answer. So please, don't lie. How many safes do you have in this house?"

"Two."

"Where are they?"

"One is in the bedroom and one is in the basement," she responded.

"Can you open them?"

"Only the one in the bedroom."

"How do you open it?"

Without hesitating, she gave him the instructions.

"What time are you expecting your husband home?"

"He usually leaves the store at six o'clock, but he might not come straight home."

"Are you expecting company?"

"My daughter could be home at any time now," Mrs. Durell replied.

"Does your husband call before he comes home?"

"Sometimes."

"Are you expecting any calls?" Rimzy inquired.

"No."

"Listen very closely. I'm going to take you upstairs and cuff you to something. Then I'm going to cuff your leg to your child's leg. They don't have to know what's going on. You can simply tell them it's a game. The choice is yours. When I put you in there, if you decide to send smoke signals or any other kind of bullshit, things are going to get crazy. If the police pull up front, I'm going to kill everybody in here, including myself. If you try to send some type of code to your husband and he comes with help, everybody is going to die. The only way things are going to work out is if you cooperate. Understand?"

"Yes," she replied, while nodding her head.

"I'm going to take the phone off the hook. So, I'm going to ask you again, does your husband call before he comes home? And if so, would he know something is wrong if he kept getting a busy signal?"

"Sometimes, but if it was busy, he would probably think our daughter was on the phone."

At that moment, Blue came in the door, removed the jumpsuit and the rest of the supplies from the box Rimzy had carried inside, and then put his wig in the box. While he was doing that, Rimzy put two fingers to his eye, pointed to her, and then pointed to the floor, which was his way of telling him without words to watch her while he went to secure the basement. He then opened the door to the basement, cut on the light, and went down the steps, all the while silently thanking Rasheeda for the pictures that made the job much easier.

When Rimzy came back upstairs, he went over to Mrs. Durell and explained that the cuffs would be removed in order to take her upstairs where the children were in the bedroom. Before doing so, Rimzy went to refrigerator to get a couple bottles for the baby and some lunchmeat, bread, and juice in case they got hungry before her husband's return.

When he came back, he told her that his partner was going to remove the cuffs from her. She seemed surprised when he made that statement. Mrs. Durell was positive that she had heard some other noise when Blue was changing, though she assumed that it was just Rimzy. The blindfold left her feeling a little disorientated.

As Blue took one cuff off, Rimzy continued to talk so there would be no doubt that other people were in the house. He knew this would further let her know there was no other option but to cooperate.

While Rimzy followed behind them, Blue slowly led her upstairs and cuffed her to the radiator in the children's room. After Blue eased out of the room, Rimzy placed the items from the kitchen on the bed, removed the blindfold from her eyes, and then told her to move her leg over so he could cuff her leg to her son's. Once that was done, he checked to make sure the cuffs were secure and that she couldn't slip out of the one on her hand. Next, he placed the items from the kitchen close to her, checked one last time around the room to make sure everything was alright, and then started backing out of the room. Before he left, he warned her to stay put and go with the program. If not, everybody would die.

Blue was waiting in the daughter's room, which was the designated spot to watch for any visitors. Rimzy entered the room and told him he had the combination to a bedroom safe, but they had to wait for the big dog before they could get inside the one in the basement.

Rimzy went downstairs to retrieve one of the 10 duffle bags they bought and then went back upstairs to the Durell's master bedroom. He went into the walk-in closet, moved a few things around, and found a small safe in the back. He flicked the dial, as she told him, and was rewarded with the 'click' sound that let him know he had been allowed entry. Inside the safe were two male Rolexes, two female Rolexes, a male and female Movado, a couple of tennis bracelets, and some iced out rings. He peered inside a small box and was absorbed by some proper tear-drop diamond earrings. A purple suede drawstring sack contained a big Figaro link and a horseshoe pendant with crazy big diamonds; it was ridiculously iced out.

Scrams must be getting it out here. Well, today isn't going to be your lucky day, you horseshoe having motherfucker. Your luck just ran out, Rimzy thought to himself.

Rimzy fumbled around and ran into some banknotes. Mr. Drug Dealer had a balance of $669,000 in his savings account, $220,000 in his checking account, and another $75,000 in a business account. In addition, there were four stacks of money. Rimzy looked through the paperwork, which contained house deeds, business licenses, car titles, birth certificates, and a whole bunch of other superficial shit he left behind. He was thinking about burning it, but then thought otherwise. He didn't want scrams to get desperate.

After his quick surmise, Rimzy put the jewels in a compartment of the duffle bag and then threw in the money. He then closed the safe and went to tell Blue what he found.

While they were waiting in Porsche's room for Mr. Durell to come home, they heard when Mrs. Durell's son woke up and were pleased when Mrs. Durell went along with Rimzy's suggestion about telling her son they were playing a game.

It was three long, painstaking hours before Mr. Durell the big drug kingpin returned home.

They had everything staged just right. The music was playing low. Blue was dressed in Mrs. Durell's bathrobe, leaning over the sink like he was doing dishes and talking on the phone. The only light on was the kitchen light. Mr. Durell came in, and after seeing who he thought was his wife in the kitchen, he shut and locked the door. Before he could turn around, Rimzy came out of nowhere and shocked him in the neck with a stun gun. Mr. Durell hit the floor and started shaking like a crack head going through withdrawal. While Mr. Durell was having convulsions, Rimzy and Blue searched him and found a 9mm. After disarming him, they dragged him to the basement and sat him on one of the metal bar stools. They cuffed his hands behind his back between the metal, and then Blue went back upstairs to check that Porsche hadn't decided to come home right then.

When Blue came back down the basement stairs, Mr. Durell was regaining consciousness. So, Rimzy took out the Desert Eagle and smacked him in the face so hard he knocked his false teeth out. Rimzy thought they were Mr. Durell's real teeth until he saw them lined up and attached to artificial gums. He smacked him again on the bridge of his nose, which started bleeding profusely, along with his mouth. He definitely knocked all of the fight out of Mr. Durell.

"I'm only going to ask you this one time," Rimzy told him. "How do you open this safe?"

They had already opened the door leading to the safe from the key on Mr. Durell's key ring.

Once again, Blue ran upstairs to check on Porsche, and by the time he returned, Rimzy was opening the safe. He looked over at Blue and motioned for him to come over to where he was standing. They couldn't believe how much money was in the safe; it was more than both of them had ever seen in their entire lifetimes.

After they recovered from the shock of seeing such an abundance of money, it was back to the plan. They removed the cuffs from Mr. Durell, dragged him to the other side of the basement, and cuffed him to the flat bench of the universal machine he had bolted into the floor. From there, Blue went back upstairs, while Rimzy started filling up the bags. Rimzy was on some *Laverne and Shirley* bottling plant operation mode. Take money from safe, put in bag, take money from safe, put in bag...He continued the process over and over, until the safe was empty and eight of the ten bags he brought were filled with multiple stacks of dead presidents.

By now, Rimzy was exhausted. He sat down to catch his breath for a minute after he finished zipping the last bag closed. Sweat was pouring off his face like he had just finished squatting 405 pounds in the big yard. With those thoughts, he hoped scrams didn't bring in some export DNA cats to analyze the puddle of sweat that seemed to disintegrate into the plush carpet.

No slip-ups, Rimzy thought, as he took a rag out of his pocket and wiped his face. After placing the rag back in his pocket, he snatched up two bags and made his way up the stairs. He got himself in the rhythm of repeating this new process until he had all of the bags upstairs. Then he coughed and Blue materialized, responding to the signal. When Blue came down the stairs, he noticed how Rimzy had packed all of the bags. Everything was completely unorganized and the bags sported several lumps.

Blue worked at the 24-hour Pathmark on 125th Street part-time at night to collect some extra ends around the holidays so a few bonus gifts could be found under his tree for his children on Christmas morning. Often times, there wasn't a lot of work to do, so his boss issued him the duty of packing bags once he finished his clerk duties. If there was one thing he learned from packing bags for three months, it was that organization was the key. He found that if he situated things, he could have a lot more room to work with.

Blue told Rimzy to go hold the window down, while he restructured the bags. After about thirty minutes, Rimzy heard the cough. When he got downstairs, Blue was standing proudly next to four full bags and one partially full bag. Blue explained that the fifth bag was about half full, but he put all of the other empty bags in it, also.

They waited an additional forty minutes until some lights pulled into the driveway. Porsche got out and then the lights backed out of the driveway. Once Porsche came into the house and shut the door, Rimzy stepped out with his pointer finger to his lips and the Desert Eagle in her face. Blue then came up behind her, guided her to the stair banister, cuffed her hands, and put a gag in her mouth.

They were getting ready to leave, but something didn't sit right in Rimzy's stomach. He went downstairs and saw that Mr. Durell was still cuffed to the universal machine. He then came back upstairs, went to the kitchen to look in the cabinet, where he removed two bottles of bleach. Next, he went back downstairs, walked over to the spot where he had been sweating, and poured both bottles around the whole area. When he finished, he took the two empty bottles and rubbed them around in the wet area. He then walked over to Mr. Durell.

"I could kill you right now," Rimzy said in the most menacing voice he could muster up. "But you gave me no reason to. I saw your banknotes. You're still a very rich man. I know you got some work stashed around here. I would advise you to stop selling drugs and go one hundred percent legit, because one of the universal laws of life is what goes around comes around. As long as you do dirt, you're going to get dirt. And believe me; it could get a lot worse than this. Do you understand?"

"Yes."

"Now I'm going to tell you something, and this might be the most important thing you hear in your life. I went out of my way not to harm your family. If you go to the police, I guarantee you--" He paused to make a long kissing sound. "On my word as a man, you and everything you love will die painful deaths. Oh, I saw those deeds you have in Raleigh, Hartford, and Newport News. I also found the addresses of certain loved ones in your fancy state of the art rolodex. You could run, but I can guarantee a lot of people are going to get caught. Our beef ends here, if you let it. But if you push the issue, and I hear about you asking questions, trying to play gangsta"— He made the kissing sound again. "Am I understood?"

"Yes."

When Rimzy snatched two more bottles of bleach out of the kitchen, Blue looked at him with a lost expression on his face. Rimzy whispered in his ear to pour the bleach all over the area where he had fixed the bags, while he went upstairs to pour it by the window they had used as a look out. This must have been a paranoid, schizophrenic move on Rimzy's behalf, but Blue went with the program; no slip-ups.

While Rimzy was upstairs, he checked on Mrs. Durell, who was watching TV and holding the baby.

Once they were done removing any possible stains of DNA, Rimzy told Porsche, "Here is the key to the cuffs," and placed them on a table in the living room. "Your father is in the basement. Before you do anything stupid, I would seriously advise you to go to him and let him handle the situation. Do you understand me?"

Because the gag was still in her mouth, she responded by nodding her head.

He then placed a small steak knife in her hand. No words needed to be said. She knew the knife was to cut through the banister. They both also knew it would take at least a half an hour for her to get free.

After his instructions were given, they snatched up the bags, walked out the door, locked it, and hit the alarm on Mr. Durell's 750 BMW. They put three bags in the trunk and two in the backseat. The windows were tinted, so nobody could see inside. Blue was driving, so

Rimzy got into the passenger's seat and put the Desert on his lap. Ride or Die. When Blue cut on the car, the Drake's "Successful" came through the speakers.

Blue slowly eased out of the driveway and drove the five blocks to the Wal-Mart parking lot. Once he neared it, Rimzy got out and Blue drove off, driving about ten more blocks down to the high school, and parked next to the track behind the bleachers. Two minutes later, Rimzy came from the other direction, pulled alongside the BMW, and they quickly transferred all the bags from the BMW to the van. They chose not to make the switch at the Wal-Mart was because the parking lot of the store was under security video surveillance and cameras were poster around the entire outside perimeter. They were definitely not trying to be seen. No slip-ups.

After the transfer was complete, Blue jumped in the BMW and drove in one direction, while Rimzy drove in the other. Blue drove three blocks to a secluded residential neighborhood, parked toward the end of the block, got out, and started walking. When he turned the corner, he walked a few steps, looked around, and then jumped into the parked van.

As soon as Blue was inside, Rimzy pulled off and drove toward the highway. While he was driving, Blue removed the jumpsuit, wig, and make-up. A few stop signs later, Blue was driving and Rimzy was in the cut. Once again, there wasn't much talking during the drive. Both men were emotionally and physically exhausted. They were running on pure adrenaline. About five hours into their trip, the sun started to rise and the highway hosted an influx of cars; mostly working people making their commute to work. It wasn't until they finally crossed the George Washington Bridge entering Manhattan and then the Bronx that Rimzy started to relax. He was nowhere near total calm, but it was a start.

When they pulled up in front of the Honeycomb Hideout, Rimzy hit the sliding door hard, handed Blue three bags, and grabbed the remaining ones. After locking the door behind them, they were relieved of an enormous amount of tension.

MISSION COMPLETE!

Chapter 11

Before they left to commit the jux, Rimzy rented a furnished basement apartment in a private house way uptown. Only thing he brought was a big safe to put the money in once they came back. As Rimzy made his way from the car to the door of the apartment, his mind flashed back to his welcome home party, where he had brushed Rasheeda off when she tried to bless him with the idea. Back then he thought that she was just a little girl trying to start trouble. Now he was sure that she was a rider; definitely inner circle material. He thought, *She's got a few stacks with her name on it for sure!*

As soon as they entered the house, they didn't waste any time. After taking a seat at the fold-out dining table with two chairs, Blue opened one of the bags and started stacking the paper, which took up the whole table.

"This isn't going to work," Rimzy told Blue.

Then he walked over, spun the dial on the safe a few times, and opened it. From there, he told Blue to transfer the money on the table to the bed. While Blue was doing that, he looked in the cabinets for a couple of pens and paper.

"This is how we're going to do this," he told Blue. "We're going to count off stacks of one hundred G's. Once we got a stack, we're going to put it in the safe and mark it down."

It was an ugly, long, tedious process, but when it was all said and done, they had $4.3 million in cash, plus the jewelry.

Once they placed it all in the safe, Rimzy turned to Blue with a serious look and said, "Alright, let's count it one more time just to make sure."

Blue looked at him like he was crazy, and then they both started laughing. They were laughing out the frustration that had seeped into their bones over the last couple of weeks. They were laughing so hard, tears came to their eyes. Once they released all of those emotions through laughter and tears, they were even more drained.

Since they hadn't eaten anything all day, Rimzy asked, "Do you want something to eat? I'm going to run and get some food."

"I could go for some Soupbowl," which was a Caribbean restaurant that served the best ox-tail or curry goat in the Bronx.

By the time Rimzy came back, Blue had taken a shower and was sitting on the bed in his shorts and a t-shirt. He had left an overnight bag there because he knew after being on the road in that get-up, the first thing he would want to do is change.

While Rimzy was gone, he made a call to Sanae to see if the P.O. came through, and she told him no. He contemplated calling his moms, but decided to wait until the next day.

Blue noticed that beside the food bag, Rimzy also had a brown bag.

"A little celebration is in order after we eat," Rimzy said, after handing Blue the bag, which contained a bottle of Hennessy Black. Next he pulled out a pack of Backwoods and a fifty of Kush

After they ate, they poured some liquor, and Rimzy made a toast. "To the world and everything it has to offer."

"Bang, bang," Blue said in response, and then they clanged glasses.

Soon, the hideout was fogged out and they were in there talking shit. They planned on leaving, but those forty plus hours they had been up, combined with the Henny and earth smoke, had changed all of that. They went to rest about 1:00 a.m. and woke up about 6:00 p.m. the next evening, after sleeping a whole fifteen hours.

Rimzy opened his eyes, laid there for a couple of minutes, and then got up to brush his teeth, and shower. When Rimzy came out of the bathroom, Blue was just sparking an Backwood. Rimzy sat across from him at the table and they started vibing.

"I got a way to put some of this paper on the books," Rimzy told Blue. "While I was up north, I read this book called *How to Start an Independent Label*. Basically, I know how to start an independent music label."

Rimzy then proceeded to break down all of the particulars on how they could get the label started with short-ends.

"Once we get the label, I know a spot that could make a thousand CD's professionally, with our jacket and all of that, for a thousand dollars. We sell the CD's for ten dollars a pop and make ten G's on the books. If we spend ten thousand, we'll get a hundred thousand back on the books from selling off all the albums. I figure we give the artists ten thousand off of every hundred. Give the government thirty for taxes, and we get sixty on the books clean. I say we get three artists. If each of them sells thirty-five thousand CDs apiece, we will have a clean six hundred thousand. We might have to spend a few G's on studio cost, a little cock-off office, and a few promotional parties, but in the long run, it will be on the books. Shit, you never know, the CD's might start selling. If that happens, it's over."

"So, you're telling me that we'll have to kick out a million to get back six-hundred thousand on the books, and with three-hundred thousand a piece on the books, we could open up other businesses and keep making clean money. I'm feeling you, cuzzo," Blue responded.

"I really want to do this right and see if we could make good music. So, I feel we should both go to this music engineering school in the village," Rimzy suggested. "It's a four-month course. I feel we could meet some good connects in the school, plus get a better grasp on how to make our music so we can launch our record company. The CD's might not sell; and I'm not trying to pay producers royalties on some bogus shit. I want Producer, Executive Producer, and Publishing credits. The only way we're going to be able to do that is if we know the game. Basically, what I'm trying to say is that we have to lay low for a few months. No reckless spending of paper; nothing major where the Feds will come in and start investigating us before we can lay down our music plan.

"I know you're going to cop a whip. As a matter of fact, I'm going to get one tomorrow under Sanae' name. Also, Mama Bear got this real estate lady friend. She told Mama Bear all she needs is ten G's and she would co-sign a lab for her. What I'm going to try to do is tell Mama Bear to give her forty thousand dollars under the table. The real estate agent can keep ten to say Mama Bear gave her ten and that she put up twenty thousand out of her own pocket for a three-family house. This way, I could live in one on the low and lace it something decent, but tell my P.O. I'm living upstairs with Mama Bear. She could rent out the other two apartments, and that should cover the mortgage, heat, and electricity. This way, the house is paying for itself on the books. Other than that, I'm going to give Black twenty thousand and tell him to breathe easy. I got to give my brother's lawyer twenty-five thousand. I'm also going to give Sanae twenty-five thousand: twenty thousand to hold for the whip and five thousand to trick on herself. Let me add this shit up." Rimzy paused so he could do the calculations. "Damn! That's eighty five thousand off the top I'm walking out of here with."

"No, you're not," Blue said. "You take care of your brother, and I'll take care of mine. Take off that twenty grand for Black. You pay the twenty-five for your brother's lawyer, and I'll give Black twenty. If he needs more, he can get it, but I'll be damned if he's going to be running around spending crazy cake if I'm going to be on a budget."

"Hold up, Blue," Rimzy interrupted. "Listen, baby boy, we ain't got to be sitting here squabbling over no G's. We rich; we got millions. I'm going to give Rasheeda two hundred thousand and see how she handles that, but she ain't getting that any time soon because I don't want her to blow her spot up down there."

"Basically, we got two mill a piece."

With that, they walked over to the safe.

"The top three shelves are yours, the bottom three is mine, and the heat is in the middle. Keep track every time you take some cake. I'm going to leave a pen and paper in the safe. This way, you won't lose count," Rimzy said, and with that, he started pulling out stacks, removing one hundred thousand dollars. "You can piece Black off with whatever you have for him now. Tell him I got him."

While taking out seventy-five thousand, Blue asked, "Yo, are you going to get your whip tomorrow?"

"Yeah," Rimzy replied.

"What kind of whip are you copping?"

"A Yukon Denali. What about you?"

"I think I'm going to fuck with a Navigator. Check it, after we cop, let's go do a little shopping."

"No doubt," Rimzy said. "Matter of fact,"

He went into his wallet and found the card that the owner of a rim and car stereo shop gave to him a while back with his number. He told Rimzy whenever he got his whip to make sure he went to get it tightened up over there. Rimzy wrote down the address, gave it to

Blue, and told him to meet him there after he copped his whip so they could lace their rides with TV's and such.

"No doubt," Blue said, and with that, they snatched another twenty-five thousand, marked it down, and closed the safe.

After placing the tablecloth and TV on top of it and straightening up the lab a bit, they left.

Chapter 12

They put some pep in their step on their way to the van because it was raining. Rimzy opened the door, hit the switch so Blue could get in, and then jumped in the driver's seat. WBLS was playing "Cherish the Day" by Sade.

Rimzy turned to Blue and asked, "Do you think it's a coincidence that this song is playing?"

"I don't know," Blue responded, "but this day will always be cherished."

With that, Rimzy slowly pulled off.

When they got to White Plains Road, Rimzy said, "I got to call Mama Bear and Sanae right quick."

Blue was getting ready to call Nay-Nay and tell her that he was on his way home and to ask if she needed anything. But then he realized her shift at the hospital wouldn't be over until midnight.

Black's baby mother answered the phone after the second ring.

"What's up?" Rimzy asked her. "Can you put my mother on the phone?"

"Can you call back in ten minutes, because I'm on the other line?"

Rimzy felt like spazzing out on her, but he showed tolerance, "What I have to say to her will only take ten seconds."

She sucked her teeth and reluctantly passed the phone to his mother.

"Hello," Mama Bear said.

"Listen, Ma. I'm coming to get you. I'll be there in twenty minutes."

"Alright, I'll be ready."

His next call was to Sanae.

"Hello, sweetness. I thought you were coming home last night. I was worried about you."

"I'll be there in a few. So breathe easy," he told her.

"Okay," she said.

The rainy streets ahead of him were illuminated by a glittery sea of rear brake lights, as Rimzy drove toward the Bruckner Expressway so he could drop Blue off.

When he pulled up in front of Blue's lab, Blue turned to him and said, "I'll call you about one o'clock once I vibe with Nay-Nay after she gets home from work. I'll confirm about us meeting at nine o'clock in the morning at the rim spot. There shouldn't be any problems. You know the saying: money talks, bullshit walks."

On that note, they shook hands, hugged, and then Blue made a dash toward his building.

During the short drive over to Prospect to pick up his mother, Rimzy had all kinds of thoughts running through his mind. By the time he knocked on Coco's door, his mind was focused on getting his moms her own lab. His mother opened the door, ready to go.

"Ma, bring those legal papers Ramel sent you."

"Okay," she said, and then went to get them. Upon her return, she asked, "Are you going to see the lawyer for him?" Before answering her question, Rimzy said goodbye to Coco and shut the door behind him, not wanting her in his business. "Yes, I'm going to go see what he's talking about tomorrow. What do you feeling like eating?" he asked.

"I just ate, baby," she responded.

"Well, do you need to make any runs or anything while I'm here?"

"No, I'm alright."

He knew his moms had an ice cream fetish, so he started driving towards Carvel's. When he pulled into the lot, he cut the van off and went into the whole beat about her real estate lady friend. When he finished, his mother just looked at him.

"Please, Ma, don't hit me with no speeches. The opportunity came for me to make some serious money, and I took it. I couldn't just sit back and let Coco dictate anything to you or let the children be divided up all over the place. My money wasn't even right enough to go see the twins, let alone deal with the fire. Now we are all in a better place, and if this lawyer does the right thing, Ramel could be coming home."

"All of that sounds good, Rimzy, but what if things didn't work out? All I got is you out here that I can truly depend on. If something happens to you--"

Rimzy reached over and hugged her as she started to cry.

"Nothing is going to happen to me. What happened was a thousand miles from here in another state, and that might as well be another country. Nobody is looking for me. It's over. So, you don't have to worry. Everything is going to work out just fine."

With those words of comfort, Mama Bear started regaining her composure.

After a few moments of silence, Rimzy pulled out six stacks of paper, each consisting of ten thousand dollars.

"Here, put this up. It's sixty thousand dollars. Each stack has ten thousand in it. Give your friend forty thousand and put the other twenty thousand up somewhere safe. That is for any loose ends you might have to straighten out, plus to get knick knacks for the apartment. Ma, put all the major purchases on your credit card or the department store's credit plan, and defer the payments for as long as possible. I don't want to throw up any red flags and risk being investigated because of suspicions of where all this money is coming from. In a few months, I'll be on the books legitimately, but for now, we have to be easy. Don't get me wrong; I want you to get the finest furniture you can find and the biggest TV in the living room for the children. Y'all deserve it. Just make sure you get those deferred payment plans.

"And, Ma, don't tell anybody my business, not even the children. Just tell them you hit the numbers or something. You still playing 677?"

She smiled in response.

"Also, give Coco a thousand to pacify her until you get out of her house. Even though I'm thankful for her letting you stay there, I don't appreciate the way she's been treating you."

After their talk, they went into Carvel, where his mother ordered a pint of pistachio ice cream and Rimzy ordered a little cake for Black's children.

Twenty minutes later, after dropping his mother back off at Coco's, Rimzy walked into Sanae's lab. He immediately got down to business, explaining her part of the plan.

"Check it. I want you to know that I appreciate everything you've done for me after the fire. To be honest with you; I came into a lot of money. I don't want to get into specifics, but I will tell you, you don't have to look over your shoulder when you're with me. Everything is good. Rimzy pulled out a stack of money. Sanae looked at Rimzy with worry in her eyes. Here are your two G's back, and another G for renting the van," he began.

She started to tell him, "The van didn't cost a thousand," but Rimzy ignored her and continued.

"Plus, here's another extra five for looking out," he said before she could say anything, while pulling out another stack. "This is twenty thousand. I want you to cop me a fully equipped Yukon tomorrow morning. This paper isn't on the books. So, you're going to have to take however much you need to drive it off the lot tomorrow out of your account and just balance the payments with whatever is left. Basically, when you get paid, you can just bank your check and live off of the money I gave you until things balance out. I know it's going to cost more than twenty G's. Once we get everything figured out at the dealership tomorrow, I'll give you the rest."

"Listen, I want to be at the dealership first thing in the morning. Is that going to be a problem with your job?" he asked.

No, if we get out early, we could do it before the store opens. Matter of fact lets get on the computer and find out everything we need to know about Yukon's, so we'll be in a better position to negotiate tomorrow". Rimzy was feeling Sanae's initiative. It's seemed like they were getting closer and closer.

Chapter 13

Rimzy and Sanae left the apartment at 8:30 a.m. on the dot. She had on her usual: a burgundy matching business skirt and jacket, with a mean charcoal grey blouse that had a burgundy skinny string draping down and tied in a bow. Then she took it over the top with the high-heel grey and burgundy stilettos, which were fitted over some grey stockings that accentuated her legs. She was definitely dressed to impress and had it going on to the fullest. Rimzy was dressed more casually in a pair of denims, some ACG nike boots, and a hoody.

The elevator was somewhat empty when they got on, but by the time they got to the ground floor, it was filled with the early morning commuters on their way to work. A little dime piece got on at the 9th floor and was side eyeing Rimzy. When Rimzy caught the vibe, he pulled Sanae closer to him and put his hand on her hip. Rimzy did this because he had crazy respect for her and he wasn't going to play her, as well as himself, by giving shorty in her building something to talk about. Sanae's hand didn't call for that.

When they got to the whip, Sanae asked if he wanted to drive, but Rimzy declined. In no time, they reached the car dealership on 49th and 12th Avenues.

Sanae and Rimzy already knew what they wanted since they searched the General Motors' website that morning. So, there wasn't much to talk about, except the price. And they didn't even get into that until they took a test drive in the fully equipped Yukon Denali. The test drive was nice; Rimzy liked being up in the air looking down at the other cars. Once they returned to the dealership, they worked out a price, the down payment, monthly payments, insurance, and other minor details. Sanae explained that they wanted to drive the V off the lot immediately. Therefore, once her credit line was checked and approved, they started prepping the V for them.

They finished doing business around eleven o'clock, which wasn't too bad. Once outside, Sanae told Rimzy that she had to get to work and would see him later that night. After giving him a kiss, she jumped into her Acura and left. Rimzy jumped in the new, shiny black Yukon, adjusted the seat, tuned the radio to Hot 97, and slowly pulled off. The interior smelled fresh like the factory.

At the light, his jam "I'm Ready" by Alicea Keys came on. He turned up the volume, while waiting for the light to turn green. He was feeling himself.

The rim shop was only about a mile from the car dealership. Rimzy had no problem finding it and pulled right into the shop. The first thing he noticed when he got inside was a buggy-eye, special racing edition, AMG Benz. The shit had the ill rims on it, as it was sitting just as pretty as can be. Rimzy jumped out of the Yukon, with the fresh temporary stickers on the back window, and was greeted by a young black man who complimented him on his choice of vehicle. Rimzy didn't know at the time, but the black man was one of the owners of the rim shop. Izod introduced himself and walked into the office, where he pulled out a photo album to show Rimzy the work he had completed on a few Yukons, Expeditions, Navigators, Escalades, etc.

By the time they finished vibing, Rimzy was convinced into getting four piped-out custom captain chairs, plus a piped-out three-seater for the back, all black with the platinum pipes. He ordered three TVs. One was the state-of-art flip out Alpine touch screen that actually controlled the entire system: DVD, Playstation, surround sound, CD, and radio. The other was a 13-inch plasma that dropped out of the visor in the front passenger's chair. The last was a drop down 26-inch screen plasma; it was so big that they had to hook up two cameras behind it to feed a picture to the rearview window. Somehow four speakers were to be hidden in the front dash, four in the doors, and six in the back. When it was all said and done, twenty thousand dollars worth of special features were added.

When they finished going through the details, Izod told Rimzy that he wanted him to meet their security advisor Raheem. Upon meeting, they immediately shook hands, and he escorted Rimzy to his office. He explained to Rimzy that he specialized in armor placement, turbo modifications, tints, rims, stash boxes, etc. He then explained to Rimzy that the whole V didn't have to be bulletproof, only the doors and windows. He told him that he would need the five doors and eight windows done. In addition, to show Rimzy that he was on the up and up, plus to enable his customer to feel secure with the work, Raheem assured Rimzy that he would let him bust two shots in any designated area and would fix the damage without any cost to him.

By the time Rimzy finished with Raheem, he had a bulletproof V, special exhaust system, four 24-inch chrome rims, a special GMC turbo expansion kit, including headers and two stash boxes. These additions were another twenty-five thousand dollars. Raheem explained that all of the additions to his V were confidential Raheem told him that he would begin the work on his V as soon as Izod was finished, and he could pick it up in two weeks. Rimzy wasn't feeling the wait, but when they finished, it would be well worth it.

When Rimzy came out of the office and into the shop, he spotted a brand-new champagne Escalade that had a temporary sticker in the back. He knew it was Blue in the spot, probably talking to Izod. After about a forty-five minute wait, Blue came out, telling about how he had just spent thirty-five G's. Rimzy told him not to sweat it because he had spent forty-five. They laughed as they walked out the doors.

They walked to the corner and hailed a cab, which they took to 56th and 6th to have lunch at Benihana's, *the* place for off-the-grill food. It was there that Blue told Rimzy that he was going to the Bahamas to be with Nay-Nay for seven nights.

"I went to the travel agent last night. I just gotta go and pick up the tickets when we get back," Blue said.

After they ate, they walked down to 47th Street between 5th and 6th, the Diamond District, and did a little window shopping. From the Diamond District, they made the best of 5th avenue making stops at the top tier luxury retailers. Rimzy and Blue first hit up the Gucci store where they splurged on lavish gifts for Mama Bear and Sanae, as well as footwear for themselves. They continued to Louis Vuitton, where Blue copped a pair of pants with the matching jacket, and Rimzy picked up a sweat suit and a very plush, very expensive robe for himself. Rimzy found himself repeatedly picking out matching garments for Sanae. He thought about how she held him down during his hard times and decided that she deserved all of it and more. Rimzy along with Blue continued down the infamous high-roller strip, strolling in and out of all of the 5th Avenue stores, from Cartier to the Gap, picking out things here and their for themselves and their loved ones.

They were flooded with bags when they finally made it to the Mauri shop. A little hottie working in the spot took one look the Gucci and Louis bags and knew she had a couple of big spenders.

"Can I help you?"

"Yes," Blue replied, "I'm looking to get a pair of Gators and Lizards."

With her assistance, Blue copped a pair of two-toned sky and navy blue Gators and a pair of natural multi-colored Lizards. Rimzy copped a pair of two-toned dark purple and light purple Gators and a pair of burgundy Lizards, plus two outfits to go with each pair. Before it was all said and done, they each copped two suits and another pair of shoes, plus three hats, two pair of cuff links, and money clips. While their measurements were being taken by the store's personal tailor for alteration, the clerk informed them of a luxury car service that could get them to their next destination.. Rimzy agreed and had the clerk call for an SUV with ample space for their load. Satisfied with the days purchases, the two finished their fittings, paid, and made their way home.

After tipping the driver, Rimzy instructed him to wait, as he unloaded the first set of bags to carry upstairs. As Rimzy stepped inside the building, shorty from that morning was waiting for the elevator. She immediately scanned the Gucci and Louis bags with no shame. Two elevators came at the same time; she got in one and Rimzy got in the other. When he opened the door, he found Sanae on the phone.

"I need you to help me get the rest of these bags out of the whip," he told her.

Sanae quickly ended her conversation, grabbed a jacket to throw on over her sweatpants and t-shirt, and followed Rimzy out the door. When they got downstairs, Sanae was surprised to see the amount of merchandise he had accumulated. Rimzy told her to get the hats and shoes, while he took the remaining bags.

Rimzy felt the holes burning in the back of his head. Most of the people standing about outside were the regulars who were used to seeing Rimzy come home dressed in construction clothes.

A lot has changed from then until now, Rimzy thought to himself.

Chapter 14

The next morning Rimzy was up early popping tags. He had an appointment with the lawyer. After dressing in a sleek Hugo Boss suit, a conservative white shirt and a pair of black Bruno Magli shoes, he felt and looked ready to conduct serious business. He exited the building to the sound of the rain dropping its soft pellets onto the pavement. It had a rhythm that seemed to soothe his eardrums.

When he got to the lawyer's office, he told the secretary he had an appointment. After telling him to have a seat, she got on the phone to announce his arrival.

Two minutes later, the lawyer came out with a smile and introduced himself as Mr. Brownstone. Brownstone looked to be in his mid 50's. He wasn't fat, but had a pudgy build. His hair wasn't completely gray, but damn near. He had on a big pair of Versace glasses and was smoking a big, sweet smelling cigar.

Once they were inside the attorney's office, Rimzy handed him the paperwork his brother sent.

"Mr. Brownstone, my brother told me that you charge $2,500 just to look at a case to see if you would like to add it to your caseload."

At that time, Rimzy pulled out a knot that contained five G's.

"Here's five thousand dollars. This is to let you know that I'm very serious about getting my brother out, so please look over these papers very carefully. If I can help you with anything, please do not hesitate to contact me."

With that said, he gave Mr. Brownstone his number.

"My brother also told me that you would want twenty-five G's if you decide to take the case, and it would be my pleasure to give that to you as soon as you say the word."

While Rimzy was talking, Mr. Brownstone was filling out a piece of paper. When he finished writing, he handed the paper to Rimzy. It was a receipt for the five G's.

"That is not necessary," Rimzy told him. "I think we can do business without all of the formalities."

With that, he stood up and shook Mr. Brownstone's hand.

While they were shaking hands, they looked into each other's eyes, and Mr. Brownstone told him, "I'll get back to you in a couple of days."

Rimzy nodded his head, acknowledging his statement, and left.

Next, he drove to the collisions office to holla at his man Shabazz, who was on the phone when he came inside the office. Five minutes later, he ended the call. After they exchanged pleasantries, Rimzy got straight down to business.

"First let me say that I appreciate you breaking bread with me, but a couple of investments of mine really worked out well for me, so please give my position to the next man in line. Now my only problem is my Parole Officer. Could you tell him I still work here if he comes around sniffing?"

Shabazz replied. "No problem. You are now my inventory Supervisor and could be on any of our worksites. Here, take this." He handed Rimzy a clipboard full of inventory sheets.

"Good looking. Check it I might be trying to do a project sooner than later, you think you could put together a top notch team?" Rimzy asked.

"Soon as you're ready just get at me. I got crazy man power." The two shook hands on their agreement and parted ways.

From there Rimzy linked up with his mother. "Everything went good with Marlene, my real estate lady friend" Mama explained to Rimzy. "I tried to get in contact with you yesterday, because she gave me the keys. It's a nice three-family house on Pugsley, right off 172nd Street. The house cost $520,000, and the mortgage is $3,500 a month for twenty-five years. That's with putting down ten percent. I also took out full coverage insurance, which means they pay for any damages inside and/or outside of the house. Plus, they'll put us in a hotel until either the house is fixed or our insurance settlement is reached. What happened before will never happen again.

Rimzy nodded his head, content with the way Mama was handling her business.

"Also," she continued, "I went shopping today and purchased carpet, a living room set, a dining room set, and three bedroom sets. I did like you said, putting it on all the stores' credit plans, with minimal payments down. I set everything up in a way that if everything is paid within a year, there will be no interest. Hopefully before the year is out we could pay it off, because after that they worked out a nice, long payment plan, that will have us paying almost double." Mama said seeming content with her new surroundings.

"Ma, I hope you got top-of-the-line furniture," Replied Rimzy.

"Shit, the carpet alone cost two G's, and I got a leather living room set. Everything is top of the line, mattresses and all! The carpet people already came and took all of the measurements. They're supposed to install it first thing in the morning. All of the furniture is supposed to be delivered this afternoon. "

"I still got a lot of running around to do, son. I got to get linens, towels, pots, pans, bathroom stuff...you know, all the little things. Sunday, after all the stuff is delivered, I want to go to Costco to get a TV, stereo, microwave, DVD player, Playstations, phones, washing machine, and a dryer...basically, all of the electrical appliances. I'm going to need you, so meet me at my job Monday at five o'clock. Oh, and before I forget, here are the keys."

She gave him a ring with a lot of keys, and then explained which ones were for which doors.

"Those keys open every door in the house. So, if you decide to check the house out and I'm not around, you've got access to everything," she told Rimzy. "Once we get settled in, I'll put an ad in a few papers to fill the other apartment."

Rimzy felt more comfortable with the idea of Butter, who was the mother of his brother Ramel's son, occupying the downstairs unit of the house. So, he made the suggestion to his mother.

"Ma, why don't you try to get Butter to come live in the downstairs apartment? It would be good for the kids. Plus, we won't have to deal with strangers in the house. Tell her that she doesn't have to pay rent, but that you will have to give her a receipt for seven hundred dollars every month. The way I see it, after gas, water, and electricity bills, your overhead should be no more than four G's a month. Ma, go buy a safe, a nice fire and waterproof one, because I'm going to give you fifty G's to cover you until next year. That should cover the mortgage, furniture bills, insurance, gas, electric, water, and any other bill that comes up."

Rimzy and his mother then went out for dinner and kicked it for a few hours. During that time, he informed her that he had met with the lawyer.

When he returned home, Sanae was sound asleep. Rimzy joined her with a clear head and a positive outlook on things. He slept well knowing that he might finally be able to bring Ramel home.

Chapter 15

By the time Rimzy got up, Sanae had already left for work. He went to the bathroom and took that morning piss. Then brushed his teeth, washed his face, and walked to the kitchen to make some breakfast. On his way past the dining room, he saw the keys to the whip on top of the dining room table along with a brief note: *You looked so sweet sleeping and I didn't want to disturb you. I know you probably need the whip today, so here are the keys. Hold it down, baby.*

Rimzy smiled. Sanae was a real thoroughbred. With that thought, he entered the kitchen and made a quick breakfast. After eating and showering, he threw on a grey Enyce sweat suit with a matching Enyce long-john shirt and a pair of all grey Nike ACG boots. Once dressed, he called Black at work and asked if he could come to his lab when he got off.

When he walked out the door, the first place he went to was the Waterbed Factory to cop a bed, picking out a proper king-size waterbed with ceiling mirrors inside of the canopy. It had six draws inside the platform and lights inside the headboard. He got the matching armoire with mirrors and a mural of a lion with the end tables. The entire bedroom set was made of mahogany wood. From there, he drove to the Furniture Warehouse and purchased furniture for his living room, dining room, and two bedrooms. Next, he went to the same electronic store as Mama Bear and got the same electronic setup as his mother. Next stop, the carpet store. His mother made sure she gave him the dimensions of her set-up because they basically had the same floor plan. Rimzy told the stores' personnel to deliver tomorrow afternoon, with the exception of the carpet installers who would be coming through that evening.

By the time he finished going through everything, it was 7 p.m. He drove over to Dogman's lab, which was in Queens, where Rimzy picked up two sets of 3-week-old pit-bulls: two girls from one litter and two boys from another litter. They were all jet black red-nose purebreds. He also picked up two black Shar Pei's from different litters. Dogman was a licensed breeder, so he got all the paperwork on the dogs.

"Bring them back in two months," Dogman told him, "and I will train them, but you have to come and see them for an hour a day every other day so they will know your scent. In the meantime, bond with them and only have them around people you want them to be around. Other than that, all you have to do is have your codes ready."

Rimzy knew what that meant. The dogs were going to be security dogs. They were not only going to be potty trained, but trained to attack on command.

After paying Dogman, he loaded the car with the dog supplies he had purchased and hit Frances Lewis Boulevard, subsequently taking the Grand Central Parkway to the Triboro Bridge. Once in the Bronx, he drove to the house, put the cages and dogs in the first floor apartment.

After everything was inside, he rolled and smoked an 'L', and then bugged out with the dogs until Mama Bear and the children came home. This was the children's first time at the house, so they were open. Before they could jet upstairs with their little bags, Rimzy called them into the first floor apartment. Immediately, they fell in love with the dogs. Mama Bear thought they were cute, as well.

"I'm giving the Shar Pei to the twins when I go out there. The pits are staying here and will be our guard dogs. Rimzy explained everything that Dogman told him, to his mother.

After a few minutes, Mama Bear said to the children, "Come on, guys. Let's take these bags upstairs so we can get the rest of our stuff out of the car." Rimzy intervened, "Ma, I'll get the stuff out of the car. I know once they get upstairs, they're not trying to come back down and get the stuff."

While they went upstairs, Rimzy went out to the car parked in the driveway. As he was getting the stuff, he saw Black driving slowly down the street trying to find the house. He flagged Black down by throwing his hands in the air.

"What's poppin', baby?" Rimzy shouted out, while Black parked in the driveway. After their embrace, Rimzy said, "Long time no see. I've been trying to get at you, but I could never get in contact with you."

"Between work and going to the studio, even wifey's beefing about me not spending enough time with her," Black replied. "I've been trying to get at you, too, but you've also been on the run. And forget about Blue. He left me a message for me to get at him because it was very important. He said it wasn't any drama, so I admit it took me until the next day, but now he isn't answering his phone. I've been trying to reach him for three days."

"Blue went to the Bahamas," Rimzy informed him. "He'll be back Friday."

"The construction business is poppin' like that? Those motherfuckers at my job are working me to death, and I'm just making ends meet. Studio time is killing me."

Rimzy interrupted him, "Help me take these bags upstairs and then we can vibe."

Black was stuck when he saw how elaborate the lab was furnished. The children were already playing the Playstation game system on the 65-inch TV. Black immediately went over and gave his aunt a kiss on the cheek, while expressing to her how much he liked the place.

"Come on, Black. Let's go walk the dogs," Rimzy said, as they made their way back down the steps.

"You've got dogs?"

By then, Rimzy had opened the door to the first floor apartment, where the dogs were playing with their toys.

"Wow. Did y'all buy the whole house?" Black asked, while laughing and playing with the dogs by grabbing their mouths and shaking their heads.

"Yeah, me and Blue came up. I have some paper for you and so does Blue. The only thing you have to do is be easy with the way you spend it, because I don't want anybody putting us under any investigation."

He told Black about the lab, the whips, and all the stuff they had to go though to keep shit looking right. Black was definitely feeling Rimzy's vibe.

Before they left, Rimzy went upstairs to tell his mother to look out for the carpet installers because he was leaving. After giving her a kiss and hugging the kids, out the front door he went. Once outside, he handed Black an envelope with $25,000 inside it.

"Do you," is all he told him before they went their separate ways.

Rimzy made it to Sanae's lab at about 12:00 a.m., where she had left some fried chicken and baked macaroni in the microwave for him. After Rimzy ate, they watched a little TV and had a little ill fuck session. While they lay in the bed, Rimzy broke the news to her.

"My moms got a new lab, so I'm gonna get my parole changed over there. I really need to spend some more time with Mama and the kids. I just need to handle my business for right now. But I want for us to live together eventually. I want you to know that I appreciate how you stepped up and believed in the kid when things got funky. No matter how shit pops, our love is 100% bulletproof. Feel me? "

She simply kissed him and put her head on his chest. No words needed to be spoken.

Chapter 16

The next morning, Rimzy awoke from a pleasant dream in which his twins Geovoni and Geovonté played freely in an open field as he watched over them. It was a peaceful, beautiful dream for Rimzy. Since he made the decision to plan a trip to Texas, where the twins lived with their mother, they had weighed heavily on his mind. He greatly anticipated reconnecting with his first born. After shaking off the last bit of sleep, Rimzy rose off the bed ready to tackle the day's tasks. He dressed and began making his way to see his parole officer in order to obtain the pass required for him to travel. During the wait in the parole office, Rimzy was on the phone making reservations for a luxury hotel and car rental, the only things he purchased on his credit card.

As soon as Rimzy came home from jail, he put a little bit of money into the bank. In addition, he routinely deposited the money he made from the construction jobs that he worked. After a while, all kinds of credit card applications started coming in: American Express, Visa, MasterCard, etc. He settled for two cards: American Express and MasterCard. Once as he finished going through all the codes and ID, the package was a done deal.

From the parole office, Rimzy went to the house, played with the dogs for a few, and waited for the delivery man to come. All of the furniture and appliances were delivered and put in place by four o'clock. When the kids came home from school, Rimzy called a cab and took them to Game Stop, where they picked out several PlayStation games.

By the time they finally made it back to the house, Mama Bear was cooking, and the whole house was lit up with flavorful aromas. Without delay, the kids went straight for the 65-inch television and started ripping open games.

"Dinner will be ready in twenty minutes," Mama Bear called out to them.

Rimzy walked up to his mother, kissed her, and said, "I know you're glad to be in your own lab again calling shots."

"Tell me about it," she replied, smiling as she seasoned the oxtail stew and dumplings.

After they ate, Rimzy called the children in the room and vibed with them for about an hour. Next, he called Texas and spoke to Jewels to confirm that he would be out there about 2 p.m. with the twin's Shar Peis. Wanting them to be a surprise, he told her not to tell the twins about the dogs.

About a half-hour after the call ended, Rimzy called a cab to go to Sareena's apartment. She had called him crying about how she needed two hundred dollars for Saleena's glasses because she broke the pair she had; so Rimzy was on his way to get the full story.

Once Rimzy entered the house, he saw a kid dressed in a blue jean suit with a purple rag sticking out of his pocket; he was flagging. They looked at each other and nodded, but no introductions were made. Rimzy wasn't feeling Sareena having gang members up in her house. He thought to himself, *That shit means nothing but trouble, especially if scram's business in the streets follows him to Sareena's home where my daughter lays her head.*

Rimzy continued to contemplate the situation as he walked to his baby girl's room. He was surprised to see that her door was closed when he reached her room.

He knocked and she immediately yelled out, "Come in!" When he entered, he saw her on the bed reading a book.

"What's up, baby girl?"

She popped up. "Daddy!" She gave him a hug and kiss on his cheek.

Sareena had briefed him about the fight in school that got her suspended for a week, and her glasses, broken. Still, he wanted to hear the story from his daughter, herself.

After their embrace, Rimzy asked her what happened at school.

Saleena answered, "This girl kept running off at the mouth, and I remembered when you said anybody can fight…it doesn't take nothing to do that. But manipulation is an art that very few have mastered. I tried to avoid fighting, but my hands were forced."

Rimzy was smiling at the way his ten-year-old daughter quoted the jewel he gave her over a year ago…jewels that some grown men don't even know about.

"Daddy, I tried to pull her to the side and talk to her, I tried to understand what she was about, but she kept running off at the mouth. Basically, I had to fight. If I didn't, I would have had to deal with her mouth every day, and who knows who else would try to follow her and push me around thinking that I was a coward."

"So if you thought of everything, how did you break your glasses? Rimzy countered."

"Mommy broke them. She was all calm at the school when she found out I got suspended, but when we got home, she smacked me in my face and broke my glasses. Then she gave me a beating."

"What did she beat you with?"

"An extension cord."

"Do you have any marks on you?"

When she took off her pajama top, he saw the whelps on her back. Rimzy, whether out of sheer anger of sympathy, shed a tear. On that note, he stormed out of the room and called Sareena, who was talking to Scrams.

"Sareena, let me holler at you," he roared making it clear that he had something important to address.

"You put the whelps on my baby girl and broke her glasses by smacking her in her face…"

Sareena cut him off. "She thinks she's grown. Done got suspended and shit. She needed an ass whipping. My momma beat my ass and I am going to beat…"

Now it was Rimzy time to cut her off.

"Check this out. Don't you ever lay a finger on baby girl again! You put whelps on her back. Are you crazy? I'm going to fuck around and take my daughter from your crazy ass because I think you lost your motherfuckin' mind. She is a child and children fight. It's as simple as that." Sareena rolled her eyes and it was clear to Rimzy that she still did not understand him.

He raised the tone of his voice to secure her attention. "You didn't even ask her side of the story or nothing. You just beat her ass because them people said she did wrong. The only way I can understand you putting your hands on her is if she disrespected you or your house. Anything other than that is not an excuse for you to put your hands on her."

With that, Sareena's expression softened. Rimzy saw that he was finally getting through to her and continued in a less imposing tone.

"Listen, you are my baby girl's mother and I have love for you. If you need anything, I'm here. But, she is my baby girl, my flesh and blood, and I'll be damned if I let anybody abuse her, including you. If I ever hear of you beating her with extension cords, or whatever, we are going to have problems. The only way you are to put your hands on her is if she directly disrespects you. All of that other shit is out the window. You beat her straight up with your hands. Do we have any problems?"

Rimzy had never put his hands on Sareena; she knew that wasn't his style. However, she also knew his daughter was his heart, and he could have another woman come beat her ass. By the look in his eyes, she knew he was serious.

"Rimzy, I'll respect that."

"I want you to do one more thing. Go in the room and apologize to her in front of me. Let her know it will never happen again, and the only way you will put your hands on her again is if she directly disrespects you or your house. Understand?"

"Yes," Sareena replied.

"I would never disrespect you in front of her. That's why I pulled you to the side rather than flip on some other shit. Tell her that we came to an understanding. She doesn't need to know I had to put my foot down."

With that being said, Rimzy went into his pocket and gave her a G. He told Sareena to get two nice pairs of glasses and keep the rest for herself. That reinstated the smile on her face.

They walked into Saleena's room together and Rimzy watched as they hugged and shed a few tears. Then Sareena went to the bathroom to fix herself up before going back into the living room where Scrams was waiting.

Rimzy talked with his daughter for a few and basically let her know that under no circumstances should anybody put their hands on her. After that was covered, they talked about school.

"Being that you're not going to school for a week, I'm going to give you two books to read. You are to do two book reports for me explaining what you got out of them."

"Do you have the books with you now?" she asked.

"No, but I'll bring them to you tomorrow."

He then called a cab, and five minutes later, he was ghost.

Chapter 17

Rimzy felt blessed to be able to spend so much quality time with Sanae and his family now that he was released from jail. Furthermore, he was relieved that he now had the resources to provide for them. He was even more contented by the fact that he would soon be on his way to see the twins, but first he had to take care of some loose ends at home. Rimzy sat in the back seat of a white Cadillac Escalade from Platinum Luxury Car Service, on his way to run errands, and his mind flashed furiously from the twins to Saleena. *I have to spend some more time with my baby girl he* thought. With that, he told the driver, "After we finish hitting up these spots I'm gonna need you to drop me at Bronxdale Projects instead." The driver nodded to Rimzy in the rear view mirror, and proceeded to the first stop, the check cashing place on University.

As they drove, Rimzy enjoyed the vibe he was getting from the Female driver. She was a little brownie with long hair, tight jeans, and a tight shirt. The dispatcher told him that he was getting an Escalade, but what really surprised him was the female cabby. As they pulled off, she turned up the music and the smooth-sounding voice of Chico DeBarge came blaring through the speakers. *Just came home, out on parole; just came home, out on parole…*

When they pulled up to the destination, Rimzy got out, pulled out his bankroll, and peeled off a big-faced fifty. He knew Platinum charged forty dollars per hour, so he paid for the first hour upfront, so she wouldn't think he was trying to play her.

Inside, the check cashing he instructed the teller to, "Give me ten money orders for five hundred dollars." Once back inside the cab, he told the driver to go to the newsstand on 161st Street and Jerome Avenue. On the drive over, Rimzy filled out the money orders to the nine people they were being sent to for their commissaries. He planned to give each of his boys five hundred dollars, and his brother one thousand dollars.

When he got to the newsstand, Rimzy snatched up ten copies of *Don Diva*, *Striaght Stuntin'* and *Black Enterprise*.

"Next stop is the post office on Jerome Avenue," he told the driver as he got back in the car. On the ride over, Rimzy organized the letters that he had previously written to his boys locked down, letting them know that the town was beautiful and he was enjoying his freedom. He had also written his brother a little something, telling him that he would send flicks soon and if he needed anything to get at him because he was doing well. When the cab reached its destination, Rimzy grabbed the neat stack of letters and made his way in.

After waiting in the long line and finally making it to the counter, he requested nine boxes and nine address forms. He filled out the forms, placed each brown bag in a box, paid the clerk for shipment and returned to the cab, where the driver was reading the *Don Diva Magazine*.

The next place was to the Black Liberation Store on 132nd Street and Lennox Avenue. There he copped *Stolen Legacies* by George James, which talks about how Socrates, Plato, and Aristotle—the so-called fathers of nearly every science—plagiarized the writings of the ancient Egyptians. He also purchased *Miseducation to Education* by Na'im Akbar, which talks about science and symbolism, highlighting why a lot of young black youths have low self-esteem. He thought these were two good books for his daughter. It would be a minute before she would be ready for Dr. Richard King or Ivan Dick Van Sertima. He did snatch up some videos of their seminars for himself, though.

After putting his purchases in the back seat, they were on their way to his daughter's house. When he called to say he was en route, she answered like she was bored to death.

"Hey, baby girl."

"Hi, Daddy."

"Listen, get dressed. We're going to get our hair breaded. I will be there in about fifteen minutes, so be ready."

"I'll be ready, Daddy."

When he got a few blocks from his daughter's house, he called again and told her to come downstairs. By the time she did, they were in the front waiting for her.

From there, they went to 125th Street. When they pulled up, Rimzy gave the driver another hundred dollars and told her to keep the change since they had about another forty minutes to complete his three hours.

After Rimzy snatched up his things, he and Saleena walked into the hair salon, which was basically empty. There were only three customers in the spot with ten beauticians. Rimzy walked to the back to see Hazel, introducing her to Saleena. They exchanged pleasantries while Rimzy jumped into the chair.

Before Hazel started, she gave Saleena three hair books to see what style she wanted. Rimzy told Hazel he wanted his braids swirled and tilted sideways. She had only gotten in about two braids, when Saleena popped up out of her seat, mad animated.

"I would like this style right here."

Rimzy looked at the style and had to admit his daughter had good taste. She wanted a zigzag style going straight back that looked like it required a lot of extensions.

If it was one thing Rimzy learned in prison, it was patience. So, he sat down, pulled out his *Don Diva* and *Robb Report*, and started reading them from cover-to-cover. Rimzy was just about finished reading his magazines, when Hazel announced she was done. In total, it took about four hours.

Baby girl was shining and Rimzy told her. She was cheesing from ear-to-ear, while Hazel hit her off with multiple views in two mirrors and the swiveling chair. Smiling, Rimzy looked at his daughter and thought of how she was becoming such a young lady.

Rimzy paid Hazel, tipping her one-hundred dollars for putting that priceless smile on his baby girl's face.

Hazel thanked him and they kept it moving.

Once they were outside, Rimzy said, "I know you're hungry."

"Staving is a better word, Daddy."

Rimzy had to laugh at her response. The two decided to walk up the block to Famous Seafood, where they ordered fried whiting, peas and rice and collard greens.

When they finished eating, they walked to Modell's Sporting Goods. Since Rimzy was taking her to Mama Bear's new lab, he knew she would want to spend the night with her brother and cousins. So, he told her to pick out some undergarments, pajamas, slippers, and an outfit for the next day.

Next they caught a yellow cab and headed home, happy to be spending time together.

Chapter 18

Rimzy had one more thing to put in order before he left for Texas. Since his brother, Ramel, was still locked up, Rimzy felt responsible for protecting his wife and seed. Uncomfortable with the fact that his brother's most prized possessions were on their own while Ramel remained locked up, he decided to take matters into his own hands.

Rimzy rang the bell of his sister-in-law's apartment and heard the quick flip of the peephole before the door was opened. Butter answered the door dressed in some sweatpants and a t-shirt. She was definitely a little cutie. She couldn't have been over five feet tall, with dreamy green eyes and long hair that was parted on the side and pulled back in a ponytail. She was bowlegged, and Rimzy thought she had the littlest feet he had ever seen. Her complexion was butter-colored and just as smooth. *God bless Puerto Rico*, Rimzy thought.

"Hey, big bro and little niece," Butter greeted them.

They hugged and exchanged pleasantries. Butter was not only his brother's baby mama, but they were legally married. Rimzy had crazy love and respect for her because she gave his brother 100% bulletproof love and was doing his bid with him, the way it was supposed to be done. His brother definitely had a winner.

She taught 2nd grade, so it was no surprise that Little Ramel was an honors student. He had a great coach.

Rimzy hoped the lawyer got back at him with some good news, because he did not want to see the legal system break her spirit. It seemed to him as though the legal system was formulated specifically to destroy family ties. While locked up, Rimzy and his jail mates would often discuss jailhouse politics. They reasoned that most of the prisoners in the New York Department of Corrections come out of New York City. Yet, they choose to send most of them hundreds of miles from their families to some small hick towns, which basically feed off of the prisoners' miseries like parasites.

They charge astronomical phone rates, which are the only means of communication for most prisoners to their loved ones. Furthermore, they would gripe about the fact that they would have to pay ten dollars for a half-hour's worth of phone time, on a phone line which would often times cut off in the middle of the conversation. There would often be a high connection rate charged repeatedly. Rimzy often thought, *It's a shame that a person could call Japan for less.*

"Bro, you alright?" Butter asked.

Rimzy snapped out of his zone. "Yeah, yeah...where is my nephew?"

"In the room playing that game."

Rimzy went down the hall and vibed with his little nephew for a few, getting a brief report on what was going on in his little world. Soon after, Butter came in the room and told him to wash up for dinner.

"Rimzy, are you and Saleena hungry?" she asked. "I have plenty of food."

"Nah, we're good. We just ate right before we came over. What did you cook anyway? You have the hallway lit up something special."

"Smothered lamb chops, Spanish rice, and corn."

"You're sure feeding my nephew good." He then looked at his nephew, who was seated at the table, and said, "I hope you recognize that your mother is a queen."

He nodded his head, because his mouth was full with food. When the phone rang, Butter was fixing her plate, so she asked Rimzy to answer it. "It's probably your brother."

Rimzy picked up the phone, and as sure as the sun is ninety-three million miles from Earth, it was him. After the annoying introductory message, Rimzy hit the appropriate numbers to authorize the computer to accept the call.

"Hey, baby," Rimzy's younger brother said.

"I don't get down like that," Rimzy responded. "You've been in there too long, little bro."

Ramel had to laugh. "That is a true story. What's popping, bro?"

"Well, first things first, I stepped to the lawyer and gave him the paperwork. He told me that he will get at me in a few days and let me know if he will be able to do something for us. I put a cherry on top of his reviewing fee to assure him that it would be in everybody's best interest if he could work with us."

"Good looking for that paper you sent Butter, and the food in that package was real tasty," Ramel replied.

"It was nothing. Shit is going real good for a fella right now. Did you eat all of your food yet?" Rimzy was talking about the trees he gave Butter to take him on her last visit.

"Nah, I still got mad food left. I don't eat like that."

"I hope you're washing your face. You know how you break out when it gets dirty." That was a code telling him to stay on his job because he didn't want him catching dirty urine and failing a urinalysis test.

"I'm on top of my game, big bro, but thank you for the reminder."

"Yo, I'm going to spit a couple of beats in Butter's ear so she can put a bug in your ear when she comes up there this weekend."

"She ain't coming this weekend. We have a trailer visit next week, so I told her to fall back until then."

"I hear that hot shit, big fella," Rimzy retorted with a little laugh.

"What's up with Black and Blue?" Ramel asked.

"Blue is in the Bahamas doing him for a week. I just saw Black at Ma's house yesterday. He's still working hard and playing that studio close. As a matter of fact, congratulations are in order because he told me that he's expecting a seed."

"Wow!" Ramel was truly happy for his cousin.

"I sent you some magazines and some more paper, so you got something to look out for at mail call."

"Good looking."

"It's nothing," Rimzy said, glad to help his brother.

They vibed until the standard recorded message announced that they had only one minute of talk time remaining.

"Tell Butter that they're getting ready to call us back from the yard…"

Rimzy cut him off. "Tell her yourself," he said, then passed the phone to Butter, who said a couple of uh uh's and I love you before hanging up.

Rimzy looked at Butter. "Here, take my cell number. If he needs to holler at me, hit me on the three-way." He wrote down the number and gave it to her. "You went over to Ma's house yet?"

"Not yet," Butter replied. "I've been crazy busy. But being that I'm not going to see Ramel this weekend, I'll go check her then."

"Sounds good. But, check this out." Rimzy zipped open the pocket in his sweatshirt and pulled out an envelope. "There's twenty-five G's in there. Ma is on the 3rd floor, I'm on the 2nd, and I want you to be on the 1st. We all got new furniture, 70-inch TV's, and the whole nine. I wouldn't want anything less for you. Take that paper and buy all new furniture. No disrespect to the furniture you have now."

Truth is, she kept a nice apartment, but it wasn't as nice as the items he and Mama Bear purchased for the new house.

"You were saying how your sister was looking for a new place. Give her this one, furniture and all. Also, you don't have to worry about the rent. Everything is covered."

Butter looked uneasy about the prospect. "No disrespect," she told Rimzy, "but I'm not trying to freeload off of anybody. You know how I get down."

"Listen, Butter, and listen good. I respect how you get down. How could I not? You're holding my brother down, plus when shit got funky with the fire, you stepped up full throttle and held my son and nephews down. The last thing you have to do is reinforce to me how you get down. Believe me when I tell you it's nothing. Matter of fact, just hold on to the paper until you go see my brother, and you two make a collective decision. The only thing I ask of you is not to tell anybody that I live there except my brother. Besides Mama Bear and you, no one knows that I live there." Butter tentatively took the envelope, but before she could counter his wishes, he continued."

"When you go see my brother, tell him I said don't be selling any trees up there. I know his hustling ass. I just sent him a G, so he shouldn't want for nothing up in that corny-ass spot. The last thing I want to hear is he's in the box because some lame, faggot-ass, hating dudes up there got him trapped off."

Butter listened to Rimzy. "I'll lay everything down to him when I go see him on the trailer. I want you to know that I appreciate everything you've done and are doing for us," she said once he finished.

Rimzy got up from the couch. "You're fam. I got you all day, every day, God willing."

With that said and done, Rimzy called a cab so he and Saleena could go home. After hanging up, he went into the room to get Saleena and to tell Little Ramel goodbye.

By the time he peeked out the window, he saw his ride sitting outside. Once home, the first thing he did was check on the dogs since he had just gotten them back from Dogman and they weren't used to being in the house alone yet. He and Saleena played with the dogs for about fifteen minutes before going upstairs so he could show Saleena his apartment.

"Do not tell anybody that I live downstairs," Rimzy told her. "I want everybody who is anybody to think I live upstairs with Ma, except you, Ma, the kids, and me. Feel me?"

"Not a problem, Daddy."

After they checked out his apartment, where Saleena had her own room, they finally made it upstairs to Mama Bear's apartment. Rimzy vibed with his mother for a few moments, then kept it moving to Sanae' lab. He walked to Westchester Avenue, where he caught a cab.

When he opened the door, the sweet, sticky incense aroma overwhelmed him. Sanae came out of nowhere wearing a see-thru white lacy outfit.

"Go take a shower, because I'm going to give you something to think about before you go on your trip tomorrow," Sanae told him seductively.

Rimzy came out of the shower and was directed to the bed by Sanae, who put some type of fruit oil on Rimzy and started giving him a tongue bath. She sucked between his toes, his calves, and slowly snaked her way up his inner thigh. By the time she started licking under his balls, Rimzy's Johnson was twitching.

She started stroking the base of his shaft, while licking his balls and expertly maneuvering her head, which gave her access to lick the entire length of his soul bone. She started rocking his mic like an official R&B chick.

She must have known he was about to bust off, because she stopped, shook her finger, and said, "Not yet, baby."

She then got up, grabbed a condom, and rolled it down the length of his shaft. Next, she straddled him and inserted his manhood into her dripping, wet wantonness. Sanae started off slow, but after a few minutes, she picked up the pace. Pretty soon, she was switching gears on him, while moaning and talking all kinds of freak shit.

Sanae's pussy was crazy wet. The swishing sounds compounded with the friction of their bodies were erotic.

"I'm getting ready to explode," Sanae bent down and whispered in a sexy voice, while bouncing and winding her hips.

She was sweating, but that did not stop her as she approached her climax. Soon, wild sensations started rocking her back and forth. She broke her rhythm as her pussy started vibrating. Rimzy, in his glory, watched her pleasure peek, grabbed her hips, and pushed her up and down, driving her over the top.

Sanae suddenly shuddered, convulsed, broke down, and started sucking on Rimzy's neck. Rimzy rolled over, flipped Sanae on her back, put her legs over his shoulders, and started putting in work. The love noises Sanae made only encouraged him to pump harder, his big ebony balls banging against her ass cheeks.

"I got something really special for you. You ready for it?"

"Yes, yes, yes," Sanae moaned.

Rimzy felt like his nut started from his toes and worked its way up and out of his shaft, as the condom was engulfed with a tidal wave of hot lava. Exhausted, Rimzy collapsed on top of her, and she rubbed the back of his head while he regained his composure.

After a couple minutes of snuggling, Rimzy got up to get something to drink, while Sanae went to shower. Once he finished guzzling a glass of Hawaiian Punch, Rimzy joined her.

As they were getting out of the shower, the doorbell rang. Rimzy put on a robe and looked through the peephole.

What the fuck is he doing here? Rimzy thought, when he saw it was his parole officer. He didn't like to be monitored like a child.

"Hold on a second."

Rimzy gave the house a quick scan to make sure there was no weed residue or paraphernalia. Only after satisfied with his search and informing Sanae who was at the door did Rimzy open, with a false smile.

"Hello, Mr. Green." Rimzy opened the door wide, granting Mr. Green access into the apartment.

"Greetings, Mr. Jones. It's a little late for acquaintants. In a nutshell, I was just checking up on you. It's good you're doing the right thing. I'll see you on the 28th."

While Mr. Green walked back down the hall towards the elevator, Rimzy shut the door, went into the room with Sanae, and within ten minutes, they were both knocked out.

Chapter 19

The heat hit Rimzy like a frenzy of fiends. It was hot like fire in Texas. When he walked down the steps of the plane, it seemed like it got hotter with each step he took toward the runway. When he reached the bottom, Rimzy didn't know if he was bugging out, but he could've sworn he could feel the heat from the concrete through his white-on-white uptowns.

The plane was parked at least one hundred feet from the airport's entrance, and by the time Rimzy got to the building, he was sweating bullets. He thought it was no coincidence somebody strategically placed vending machines in the airport lobby. As soon as he saw what was inside the vending machines, he knew there were some gangsters in Texas who consequently had a monopoly on the beverages. The only items available in the vending machines were Texas brand iced tea and water.

With his only piece of luggage on his shoulder the small travel cage with the Shar Pei's in one hand and a bottle of water in the other, he kept it moving out the door to a mini-van, which would transport him to the rent-a-car agency.

Rimzy coasted from the AC of the van to the AC of the agency in a couple of hop steps. There was an official red-blooded Cherokee Indian at the counter, who greeted Rimzy with a warm smile.

She cheesed hard. "Could I have your confirmation number?"

Rimzy broke the ice. "Hello, lovely lady. I guess you're the person I need to see about obtaining a vehicle that will hold me down throughout the duration of my stay in your lovely state."

After pulling out his wallet, Rimzy produced the confirmation number, his credit card, and driver's license. It must have taken Rimzy a second or two, because when he looked up, Pocahontas had already peeped his New York driver's license.

Rimzy extended his arm and handed the documents to her. The way he handed her the items, she had no choice but to touch his hand. After their brief contact, she started typing on her computer.

"Listen; tell me what's really good?"

Pocahontas was confused. She couldn't fully understand his word play. Rimzy conceded all of her doubts by stepping to his business, hard and fast.

"You look so marvelous that I would be kicking myself in the ass all the way home if I didn't try to get to know you. I'm going to be in town for a few days and I really, really hope we can link up."

Pocahontas was stuck. Most of the guys that came through the doors at her job were either too intimidated by her immaculate appearance to say anything or did not know how to come at her. She was seeing somebody, but wasn't feeling him like that. He hadn't even gotten the pussy yet. Now, here was this smooth-talking New York City guy hitting all of the right buttons.

Persia, who was 5'9" tall and 145 pounds, looked the prime age of twenty-five, like a model, and her hair, toes, and nails were on point. She only fell out of her semi-trance when one of the Shar Peis barked out loudly.

Persia looked down at a meaningless piece of paper as a diversion, and couldn't help but notice the leather caramel-colored band connected to the iced-out Bentley Breitling watch. She looked into Rimzy's eyes and peeped that his Cartier glasses complimented his watch.

Persia had only been with two men in her life and hadn't had dick in over a year. For some reason, she felt like she would be a fool not to take New York up on his offer. Without saying a word, she grabbed a piece of paper and wrote down her name and number. Rimzy didn't miss a beat. He was on it, cheesing hard when she finished writing the last number.

After thanking her for her services, Rimzy jumped into the forest green Suburban and luxuriated in the AC for a second. The first thing he did after getting inside and turning on the AC was go into his bag and pull out his CD's. He felt like something smooth, so his eyes scanned the titles until they came to rest on Maxwell's latest CD. Once he had set the music at a moderate volume, he adjusted his seats and mirrors. Then he set up his navigation system, which outlined his course. Rimzy was going straight to the twin's house. He wasn't stopping at a hotel or getting something to eat. His mind was focused on seeing his sons. Point blank. That was that genuine fatherly love.

During the fifty-minute uneventful drive to their house, Rimzy realized there was a lot of unused land in Texas. Everything was spread out. He also noticed that Texans were very patriotic, because every house had an American flag hanging in front. Most had the flagpole and the whole nine.

As he finally pulled up to the house, Rimzy was impressed with the pillars in front of the mini-mansion. The doorways and windows were a natural earth tone, the color of camel skin. The rest of the house was brick. The landscape was flooded with plenty of greenery, and Rimzy could tell the trees, lawns, and bushes were professionally maintained.

As he pulled in front of the two-door garage, one door was up revealing a pearl-white drop-top Mercedes Benz. Rimzy smiled; baby girl was doing well for herself. He knew Jewels had potential. She was always very intelligent.

It was strange how they hooked up. They knew each other three years before they even thought about being a couple. The Rodriguez family moved next door to Rimzy's family in the PJ's. From what Jewels told Rimzy, Mr. Rodriguez came from the Dominican Republic. He saved for two years before he was able to send for his family, which consisted of his wife, his wife's mother, his two sons, and his daughter Jewels, who was fifteen at the time.

It wasn't hard to tell that the Rodriguez's were doing bad, like so many others in the PJ's, despite the fact that Mr. Rodriguez worked two jobs and Mrs. Rodriguez worked one.

When the Rodriguez's moved into the building, Rimzy's father was alive and doing his thing in the hood. He had Rimzy and his family living ghetto fabulous. Three months later, his father was killed and things changed big-time around Rimzy's household. It seemed like only a matter of time before Rimzy and his brothers got caught up in the streets.

For some reason, Jewels seemed different from all of the other girls around the way. For one, she didn't hang out with the girls from the hood. That compounded with the fact that she grew up in another country gave her another kind of swagger. She was innocent, soft-spoken, and every time Rimzy saw her, she had a book in her hand. Rimzy valued his time with Jewels, because she seemed like an escape from the hood.

It was an awkward relationship because Rimzy was a big part of Jewels' life, aside from her family and school. Even when Rimzy got locked up and Jewels found out about all of his other children, she still didn't leave him.

Out of his love for her, Rimzy told Jewels to take the scholarship she was offered at Texas A&M University, but he *didn't* tell her to go and marry some doctor.

She told him that she was getting married her second year at school. Apparently, they met when he came to her school to give a seminar on cardiopulmonary resuscitation. He was a heart specialist. He offered her an opportunity to finish school and wanted to provide a home for her and the twins, who her parents were watching while she was in school. She took him up on his offer, and shortly thereafter, the letters stopped coming. Rimzy didn't want any of his children to come see him while he was in jail. So, by the time he came home, he hadn't heard a lick of news about the twins in five years.

Soon, the door opened, which Rimzy took as a good sign, and Jewels stepped through the doorway looking good. Her caramel complexion was glowing. She had on a white wife beater and a pair of white booty shorts that did every bit of justice to that bubble ass of hers.

Damn, she is a straight dime piece.

As he leaned in closer to her, they opened their arms and exchanged a big hug. Rimzy felt her heart beating one hundred miles-per-hour when they were intertwined in their brief embrace. As they walked into the gracious entranceway, Rimzy said the first words in their awkward encounter.

"You look very nice and your home is beautiful."

"Thank you. You look handsome yourself."

Her accent sounds so sweet. Hold on. Is she flirting with me?

Putting the sociology and linguistics courses (which he had taken in jail) to use, he came to the conclusion that she was flirting based on the fact that people use slang when they are in comfortable surroundings. Doctors, lawyers, judges, and bus drivers all have their own slang; they just call it jargon. Being that she reverted to such a strong accent, Rimzy assumed that she must have been comfortable with him. He knew with all of the schooling she had to go through to become a doctor, Jewel's knew how to talk proper English.

Rimzy's thoughts were interrupted when he saw the twins.

The twins were named Geovoni and Geovonté after Jewels' great grandfather and his twin brother. Rimzy was speechless. He felt the steady tears flowing down his face as the boys ran to him. The twins were eleven years old. The twins always prayed for the day that their father would come. Rimzy was on his knees and they were all huddled in a circle, crying, rubbing, and comforting one another. It took a few minutes for them to get a grip on their emotions and settle down. By that time, Rimzy was square on his ass, with both of his boys on each side of him. Once they laid eyes on the two small dogs in their travel cage, the boys went wild! After setting them free, arguing for a little while about potential names and chasing the dogs around the room, they again found themselves all over Rimzy, bestowing hugs of joy and thanks. He was beside himself with contentment.

Rimzy had been planning this trip for a minute. First, it was the money that kept him away. Then it turned into a parole issue. They were taking their time processing the paperwork that enabled him to travel out of town. After he got his pass, he and Jewels agreed he should wait three more weeks so he could come down for the father-son triathlon. The events were basketball, swimming, and bike riding. Jewels told him the events were held inside a domed air-conditioned arena. Rimzy was taking the triathlon seriously. He knew if he won at least one event it would restore a lot of confidence in the twins.

Rimzy was going to Bally Total Fitness, working out like a madman, and on weekends, Central Park was shut down to traffic to allow cyclists to train. Rimzy was out there doing laps in the park on his Cannondale lightweight mountain bike. He liked the bike he bought so much that he purchased two more and had them delivered to the twins overnight the day before.

As they sat in the living room, the FedEx truck came up the driveway and delivered all three bikes, the twins' being miniature versions of his. The twin's eyeballs popped out of their heads as they watched their father roll out the bikes.

"Thank you, Daddy," the twins said in unison.

Before Rimzy could even say you're welcome, the twins had taken off on the bikes that came pre-assembled. He had to give credit to the twins. Riding a bike around at high speeds on a 105-degree day was gangsta. Rimzy walked his bike over to the side of the house, and as he lower the kickstand, he saw Jewels in his peripheral vision waving the twins to come inside.

Her motherly instincts were on point. She knew if she didn't call them in, they would ride until they fell out. They took one more lap, and then rode up right alongside their parents. As the twins walked ahead of them, Rimzy saw a reflection of himself. They even had the same kind of swagger.

As Geovani and Geovante went straight for the refrigerator to get something cold to drink, Jewels spoke:

"Out of respect for you, I thought it would be best if my husband weren't around when you came over. You know, I see you every day in the twins, so I can't help thinking about you. Seeing you again has sparked deep-rooted feelings in me."

The rest was gibberish. As far as Rimzy was concerned, it was easy for feelings to reemerge when a person was in your face. He also knew that it was just as easy for them to forget about you once you are out of sight. Rimzy knew it was him who initially left Jewels, not vice versa. He had to do the time, not her. He also respected the fact that she had to move on. Still, he couldn't release the anger in his heart for the way she left him for dead when he was up in those mountains. She made her bed and now she had to sleep in it. It was a nice bed, so Rimzy was sure she would make out fine.

"Listen, love, I have feelings for you, too. But I've moved on to the next chapter in my life and I can't see myself going backwards."

The words seemed harsh coming out of Rimzy's mouth, but they could have been much worse. Rimzy kept his focus for a few reasons; his first and foremost reason being the twins.

There was an awkward silence as Rimzy's words lingered in the air, and no words were spoken until the sweet-tasting lemonade had quenched their thirsts.

With that out of the way, Rimzy handed Jewels a sealed envelope that contained fifty thousand dollars and then told her that he was taking the boys to ride the go-carts.

Both boys jumped in the back of the rental and automatically put on their seatbelts. Rimzy smiled because he knew that jumping in the back was a reflex for them, and must have been the way they traveled when they were with their mother.

Although Rimzy had already programmed the navigation system, he asked the boys to direct him.

"Make a right!" the twins yelled in unison.

Them speaking simultaneously messed Rimzy's head up, but the twins shook it off like it was nothing.

"I noticed the two of you didn't look surprised when you both made that last comment. It seemed like you were in each other's thoughts."

"We do that all the time, Dad," Geovani said.

"That's nothing," Geovonté added. "One time Geovani was in trouble fighting three Mexicans. They had him on the floor kicking him. I swear to you, Dad. I felt a sharp pain and knew my brother was in trouble. I ran from the game I was playing to the other side of the arcade. Somehow I knew exactly where he was and that he was in pain! We just have a connection!"

Rimzy's heart dropped to the floor. He was ready to get out an M-16 and murder anyone's entire family tree if they even thought about doing anything to his boys. He could see himself in the desert with a few militants, out for blood.

Rimzy thought about how easily the twins had gravitated toward him, and then he flashed back to how the boys jumped in the back and put on their seatbelts. It was their mother's conditioning that made them do that. Now he wondered what his conditioning could make them do.

* * * * * *

Rimzy sat on the plane in deep thought. He was overwhelmed with the fact that the twins communicated with each other on a higher plane of understanding. He had studied some kinetic sciences, focusing in on metaphysics. However, this was more on the telekinesis side. When he returned home, he was going to make sure to go to the new library they built on Fordham Road in the Bronx to read up more on the subject.

Chapter 20

Once back in New York Rimzy got a call from Izod—from the auto shop—who told him that the cars were finished and ready to be picked up. Rimzy hung up and called up Blue who had apparently gotten the call too and was ready to go down there immediately.

Rimzy and Blue met up on Westchester ave and caught a gypsy cab downtown. Once inside the shop, they were ushered over to their trucks, which were both in the air on lifts. Izod started off by showing them the new exhaust system they installed. From there he popped the hoods and showed them all of the engine modifications. Next he showed them how to use the Radio/DVD/Navigation. Everything was touch screen. Izod put a movie in and all the screens were crystal clear. Next he put the radio on and Trey Songs "think I invented sex" came thumping out of the system clear as a bell with no distortions. Rimzy wasn't the kind of fella to be coming down the block with the system booming; that was some late 80s shit, but it was good to have if he wanted to act up at a picnic or a beach. After Izod finished breaking down all of the audio visual components, he showed them how to operate their stash boxes. Each truck had two.

When all of the interior business was complete, Izod walked Rimzy and Blue to a small Plexiglas chamber inside of a bigger Plexiglas chamber. Soon the trucks were brought into the bigger chamber. Izod explained, "The way I am is the way a lot of my customers are. I want you to feel 100% secure in your vehicle and the only way I could guarantee that is if you see it with your own eyes. With that said he opened a draw and pulled out a 357 revolver and made a gesture for Rimzy or Blue to test its authenticity. Blue being a military vet snatched up the heat, hit a button that released the cylinder, took out a bullet, looked at it, then nodded his head in a slow up and down movement, while puckering up his lips; an official co sign move. Blue didn't say a word, yet everybody knew what he meant. He smacked the cylinder back in, turned toward the trucks and dumped all 5 rounds into them. The way Blue did everything all in one motion also let everybody know that he definitely knew how to handle a weapon. As soon as Blue put down the gun everybody walked over to survey the damage and was happy to see none. Everybody left the test room with smiles. Rimzy and Blue did not have a problem breaking Izod off with that paper soon as they got in the office, money well spent.

Rimzy and Blue came out of the shop back to back. Soon as Rimzy cut on the engine, he heard and felt the difference from the factory version. Once he started driving he experienced it. They were flying down the west side highway like they owned the streets. Rimzy was enjoying the engine modifications so much that he didn't even have the radio on; he was just vibing to the engine, until they made that left on Canal Street. He put on hot 97 and "Run This Town" by Jay, Rhianna and Kanye just came on. Rimzy couldn't help himself he was making it the 80s for the day, because he had that subwoofer knocking.

He spent the rest of the day riding around, handling business and enjoying his whip.

At about 6:00 p.m. Rimzy's phone rang. It was the lawyer's secretary. As soon as she confirmed that she was speaking with Rimzy, she transferred him directly to Brownstone.

"Hello, Mr. Brown. I have some news for you concerning that matter we discussed. If you're not busy, I'll be in my office until eight o'clock this evening."

"I'll be there in fifteen minutes," Rimzy replied, then hung up.

Rimzy pulled up to Sheridan Avenue, jumped out of the Yukon, and entered Brownstone's office. He introduced himself to the secretary, who announced his arrival. A minute later, Rimzy was directed to enter the attorney's office. Once inside, Brownstone shut the door. He had a sweet smelling cigar in his hand, which he waved in the air as he talked.

"I've done some research on your brother's case and we have some good news and some bad news. I always start off with the good news. The good news is your brother's arresting officer, who headed the investigation, is currently suspended without pay for shooting an unarmed civilian and planting a throw-away gun on him. His partner was interrogated by internal affairs and confirmed that the gun was in fact planted by the officer. That piece of information could be very helpful in getting his conviction overturned. Now the bad news…these two witnesses." He opened a folder and had each of their pictures inside. He then removed the two pictures. "They introduced some very damaging testimony during his trial. Basically, Mrs. Stanford and Mr. Jones testified that they heard some popping noises and saw your brother running across the street. Those statements placed your brother at the scene."

Rimzy leaned in closer, intrigued by what he was hearing. Brownstone continued, "That testimony, compounded with the fact that the victim was under investigation for murdering your other brother constituted the motive. Now this is where it gets tricky. In her initial written statement, Mrs. Stanford said she heard a loud popping sound and saw a man run across the street and down the block. However, when she testified before the grand jury, she said that she saw a man run across the street and jump into a dark colored car that sped off."

Rimzy remained riveted as though the fate of his brother laid within this mans next words.

"I'm making a big deal about these seemingly minute details, because within them lie discrepancies."

Rimzy was beginning to see where Brownstone was going with this. He listened as the story continued to unfold.

Brownstone went on, "The second witness, Mr. Jones testified three weeks later that he saw your brother get out of a dark car with a bulge in his pocket on Pleasant Avenue, precisely twenty minutes after the shooting. Mr. Jones' story is countered by the fact that he was placed in police custody for possession of 250-grams of powder cocaine and carrying an unregistered Glock pistol when he gave his testimony. He was essentially guilty of 2 Class B felonies, carrying a maximum of eight-and-one-third to twenty-five years for each charge. Ironically, despite the significance of his offenses, he copped out to a three-to-nine for both charges, in a deal that was brokered by Homicide Detective Duwit in exchange for testimony against your brother.

Rimzy was torn between hope and disgust for what he had just heard.

"Now, the way I see it, I don't think the testimony of these two witnesses is truthful. I think they were both coerced into playing Officer Duwit's game. If my investigator can get them to sign sworn affidavits that they weren't sure about their testimony and were coerced by Officer Duwit and his criminal nature, I think I can get your brother's conviction overturned. Once I get him down, I think I can persuade the District Attorney to dismiss the indictment because those two witnesses and Officer Duwit's testimony are basically the backbone of the DA's case. Now, with those affidavits and the criminal proceedings being brought against Officer Duwit, all their credibility will be shot, and that should be more than enough evidence to establish reasonable doubt if we have to go to trial."

Rimzy gave the lawyer a firm nod to establish that he understood the magnitude of work required to secure even the slightest chance at freeing his brother.

"Now, Mr. Brown, I want you to know that I'm going to charge you twenty-five thousand dollars to get him down, and if we go to trial, I'll need an additional one-hundred thousand dollars. Plus, I need to be reimbursed for all expenses, including any expert witnesses and private investigators. Can you handle these fees, Mr. Brown?" Brownstone asked with a serious demeanor.

"I can, but how can I say this..." Rimzy paused for a moment. "My money is not on the books."

"That's no problem, Mr. Brown. I can always say I'm handling the case pro bono on a contingent basis, which basically means you pay me, but nowhere near what I charge."

Being that Mr. Brownstone was talking about payments, Rimzy went to the inside breast pocket of his jacket, pulled out an envelope containing twenty-five G's, and passed it to him. Brownstone took the envelope and put it in his inside breast pocket without counting it. Eye contact was kept throughout the exchange, but no words were spoken. After the exchange was complete, Brownstone handed Rimzy two folders, which contained information obtained from his investigator about both witnesses.

"Look these over and let me know when you think would be a good time to have my investigator initiate contact with them. I think they should be feeling guilty for what Officer Duwit convinced them to say."

Rimzy could read between the lines very well. Brownstone was basically telling him to look at their dossiers and figure out the best way to step to them—putting the blame on Officer Duwit—and pay them off so they would sign the affidavits and change their testimonies.

Rimzy was feeling Brownstone's style. He was smooth; so smooth that Rimzy was certain he had a file on him. He would be a fool not to know who he was dealing with.

Rimzy stood up, shook hands with him, and said, "I'll get back to you about this."

Chapter 21

Rimzy drove back to Sanae in a world of thought. His brother was coming home. Bet that! Once home, he and Sanae ate and talked for a few. After Sanae went to sleep Rimzy went to the living room, sat down on the love seat, put the file on the coffee table, opened the first dossier and began to study its contents:

- Mrs. Tabatha Stanford, age 34, address 222 Morrison Ave., #2k

- Graduated from Juliet Richmond H.S. in 1988, no other schooling

- Married John Smith in 1997, divorced 2009

- Mrs. Standford has custody of 2 children, 1 boy age 12, and one girl, age 7

- Works at the Marriott on 47th and Broadway as a customer service representative, and has been working there for 9 years

- Hours M thru F, 9 to 5, lunch from 1:00 - 2:00 PM

- Financial status: makes $35,000 a year

- Savings $20 in savings account and $300 in checking account

- Her 535 BMW was repossessed 10/1/09, she was now driving a 1998 Mitsubishi Galant

- Outstanding Dept $1500

- Medical: daughter has severe asthma, husband was delinquent on child support payments

- No criminal history

After reading her dossier a few times, Rimzy sat back, looked at her picture and did some serious brewing. After an hour, he came to the conclusion that Mrs. Stanford was living check-to-check and just got caught a little behind. Readjusting to paying all of her bills without her husband seemed to be very overwhelming, she was barely making ends meet. She seemed very much in need of some paper to put her over the hump in the road and ahead of the game.

Next he opened Mr. Jones' file.

- Mike Jones, age 23
- Address Watertown Corr. Facility
- High School diploma
- No employment history
- Financial status 0
- Inmate account fund $13.00
- Sharon Parker was sole visitor for the first 6 months
- Last visit was mother 4 months ago
- Criminal history:
  - 1/20/03: Transit Fraud Dismissed and fined
  - 3/9/04: Disorderly conduct Mist conviction
  - 6/20/04: loitering Mist conviction
  - 7/28/07: Criminal Possession of a weapon
  - 12/3/07: Felony Conviction
  - Criminal Poss. Firearm; Criminal possession of a controlled substance; Prison term 3 to 9 concurrent
- Earliest Release 12/30/11.

After reviewing his files, Rimzy could see that scrams was having a ruff bid. He went through the same meditation process as with the Stanford file. After an hour, he knew how to come at him.

That following Thursday, Rimzy was waiting by the side entrance of the Marriott in a conservative suit and tie. When he saw Mrs. Stanford coming, he called her name, gave her his best smile and asked, "May I speak with you". She looked him up and down, obviously impressed by his appearance and asked, "About what". They were standing on the sidewalk facing one another. Rimzy replied "would you mind if I took you to lunch? I've got a business proposition that I would like to discuss with you". She thought to herself, *what kind of business opportunity could you offer me Mr.?* She looked him up and down again and this time the diamond flooded presidential Rolex almost blinded her. She continued to think to herself—*what have I got to lose? Plus that walk to Papaya's on 8th ave and 37st wasn't about nothing, fuck 2 franks and a soda for $4.25*—which was all her budget allowed this week. Rimzy waited patiently while the assortment of thoughts flooded her brain. She finally answered, "OK why not, where would you like to go." They went to the Olive Garden right up Broadway to eat.

Once inside she ordered the shrimp scampi, while rimzy ordered ravioli stuffed with ricotta cheese, covered with a meat sauce. While the food was being prepared, Rimzy came right to the point. "Mrs. Stanford, I've got an envelope in my pocket right now with $7,500. I'm willing to give you it, after we finish our meal along with another $7,500 to be paid out once you have fulfilled your part of the agreement, which might not be necessary".

Rimzy definitely had her complete attention. "I know your probably thinking, what kind of scam am I up to, I assure you Mrs. Stanford that what I'm going to ask you to do is not illegal and there is no way you could get in trouble. I'm going to ask that you do not interrupt me until I explain everything to you. Then you could have your say; do you have a problem with that?" "No," she replied. Rimzy continued, "Good, first things first, here is a newspaper article from the Daily news confirming what I'm about to tell you. Detective Dewitt was recently suspended from the force, because he allegedly shot an unarmed civilian and planted a fake gun on this person. Detective Dewitt was the chief investigator in a case that you testified for. I believe that Mr. Dewitt coerced you to change your initial written statement, where you said, 'you saw a man run across the street and keep running.' You recanted that statement and instead declared that you saw a man across the street get into a black car. Now that Mr. Dewitt's criminal nature has come to light, I'm sure that it would be no problem to..."

At that point Rimzy stopped talking, because the waitress was approaching the table with their food. Once the waitress left, Rimzy told Mrs. Stanford, "I'm sure you can still listen and eat, so enjoy your meal. Now as I was saying, this is what I would like to happen. I want to send a private investigator to you sometime this week and he is going to ask you whether officer Dewitt coerced you into changing your statement. All you have to do is say yes and explain to him that you've been feeling very guilty about the events that transpired. I need for you to clearly establish that not only didn't you see the man get into the black car, but you also weren't 100% sure that my associate (when he said associate he saw her flinch) was the person you saw run by. I know that this will contradict what you said on the stand and to the grand jury, but all you have to do is say that officer Dewitt convinced you to go along with the testimony which he concocted. You see Mrs. Stanford, this way all of the blame will fall on Mr. Dewitt, who is now a known criminal. Mrs. Stanford you'll be left in the clear. Plus have a little bonus on top of it all."

Rimzy paused long enough for the proposal to sink in, then continued. "I'm willing to give you the $7500 I've got in my pocket right now, and the only thing you have to do is meet with the investigator and sign an affidavit, basically stating what I told you.

After this is done in a few months, more than likely the indictment will be dismissed. However, if it isn't, I'm going to need you to come in to testify at the new trail, at which point you will simply restate what you signed in the affidavit.

Whether or not this is necessary, I will still give you another $7,500, but only after I know the case has been dismissed or after you testify." With those last words he looked at Mrs. Stanford, put his hands up, basically saying all his cards are on the table.

"I'm not saying I would do this, but if I did, what would be my insurance that you would give me the other $7,500, and not just try to kill me?"

"Hold up Mrs. Stanford", at that moment, Rimzy raised his sleeve on his Armani suit, and consulted his 20 thousand dollar Rolex. This was a ploy to show Mrs. Stanford that he had no intention to beat her for a punk ass $7,500.

"Please, if you remember the case, my associate allegedly killed a man who killed his brother. Two lives were lost. The scales should have been balanced with that. There should be no reason why a third person should do 25 years for allegedly killing a man who killed his brother. My associate is not an evil man Mrs. Stanford. As a matter of fact we're for the empowerment of black people as a whole. The last thing I want to do is come here trying to intimidate you in any shape, form or fashion. I can assure you Mrs. Stanford, if you follow through with your agreement, you will be paid your other $7,500. No one in our association would ever try to short change you after you did your part at giving a man a second chance at life. Do we have a deal Mrs. Stanford?"

She looked him in the eye, and slowly nodded her head and said "yes." Rimzy only took about 3 bites of his food, while Mrs. Stanford ate most of hers, largely as a means to avoid looking at Rimzy while he was hitting her with the beat.

Rimzy went into his breast pocket and took out the envelope and slid it toward Mrs. Stanford. And quickly told her, "put that in your purse, you've got my word, it's all there," before she played herself and started counting it at the table. She opened the envelope thumbed through the bills and put it in her pocketbook.

To end the meal Rimzy picked up his glass and said, "To my beautiful black queens, may their struggles uplift them to their full richness." With that, they clanked glasses and drank. When he got the waitress attention again, he asked for the check. He paid, left a generous tip and they exited. During the walk back to the Marriott, Rimzy told Ms. Stanford that the investigator would be in touch.

The next day, Rimzy's cousin Rasheeda was on her way to the Watertown Correctional Facility. She had to catch Prison Bus service at 9:00 that night, to arrive at the Facility for the 8:30 to 3:00 visit. She was dressed to impress. She had on a pair of Armani Exchange fitted jeans, with a low cut white D&G top under a tailored jacket that fit her slim waist, and accentuated her round hips. She also sported some wrap around Chanel sandals with shades to match. They wouldn't let her bring her Chanel bag in, they said for security reasons because of the chain link strap, but nevertheless, she was shinning like a movie star. Her hair, nails, and feet were touched up and finely groomed.

When Mike Jones came out, he was expecting to see his ex-girlfriend who flipped on him. When the C.O.s directed him to the empty table, he went and sat down. Rasheeda was at the vending machines getting all kinds of goodies. He saw her when she reentered through the side entrance where all of the machines were located and was lusting openly. He thought to himself, *who got this bad honey coming up in these mountains to check them?* He was stuck when she stopped at his table, put the stuff down, and asked for a hug. He got up, they hugged, and Rasheeda gave him a quick kiss with those butter-soft lips.

When they sat down, Mike was at a loss of words. He thought *this must be some kind of mistake*, but Rasheeda gave him a quick reality check. "Listen, I know you don't know me, an associate of mines sent me up here to check you. I have a business proposition for you." She basically ran down the same beat that Rimzy gave Ms. Stanford, but instead of two $7,500 payments, she offered him two $5,000 payments. Rasheeda saw his face change after she pulled his card, and began to put him at ease. Listen, I understand your situation, nobody wants to be in here. I heard you got caught with mad weight, plus the heat, so I know you wasn't no derlick out there, you were doing your thing, so fix your face, you aint got 25 to life right? Listen, you smoke trees?"

"Hell yea."

"Well I got something for you." She passed him a bag of chips; inside was 3 greased up looneys, and a little extra grease on the side. It took him a few to boof all 3. He definitely wasn't a vet like Rimzy, but he eventually had the package secured.

"I left you a food package, a pair of Tims, Sneakers, and 2 Sweat-suits, between that and the trees you ballin. Now, I don't want to send the money in your account, because it might raise eyebrows, but I could drop it off at your mother's lab if you want." He looked at her, "you know where my moms live?"

"Well I don't, but my associates do and they told me to let you know they do. But don't worry, I'll be the one who gives her the money, and I'll just tell her that I just came in town and heard about the situation, and the money is what I owe you." He was listening to her, but his mind was going a hundred miles an hour. If they knew where his moms live, that means they can get at her and retaliate for him snitching on Ramel. She watched him, but let him do the math without rushing him. Rimzy changed tactics with Mike. He didn't ask him to accept the deal he told him the deal. After all the terms were laid out, Rasheeda wanted to leave, but she was told to make him happy, so she listened to his lame game, asking her to come see him again.

She gave him a couple of kisses, let him touch the titties, but she made no promises about coming back. She didn't give him her number and told him she don't take pictures, when they started taking them. Before she left she told him, "the investigator would be up shortly and I'll drop that paper off with your mom's tomorrow night." She also told him, "don't talk on the phone about business, just tell your mother an old friend came to see you, and I'm going to drop something there for you. Also, don't tell the investigators about our visit."

On her way home on the bus, Rasheeda was smiling, thinking, *Rimzy owes me big-time for this shit.*

Monday morning Rimzy called Brownstone and told him, "You can send the person to check into that whenever you're ready, everything is all good." Brownstone said, "I see, I see, I'll get back to you, once everything checks out," and hung up.

Chapter 22

A couple of months went by and Rimzy and Blue were in Engineering School doing their thing. Rimzy was patiently waiting for the lawyer to get back at him about his brother. All in all, things were moving in a positive direction. On this particular day, Rimzy sat in class focusing one hundred percent on what the instructor was saying about the engineering board.

His phone started vibrating. Only a very select few, mostly family, had the number to his cell phone. They all knew he was in school during this time, so he thought it had to be some type of emergency.

He looked at the caller ID, but didn't recognize the number. He was getting ready to let the call go to his voicemail, but decided against it. Rimzy left his books on the desk, thinking he would only be gone a few minutes, and stepped into the hallway so not to disturb his fellow classmates.

"Hello?" he demanded into the small phone.

There was somebody crying on the other end. Rimzy couldn't make out a word they said, let alone who it was.

"Calm down. I can't understand you. Who is this?"

With those words, Sareena took a deep breath and said, "Saleena has been hurt. She's at Jacobi Hospital. Come now. We need you."

When Rimzy asked what happened to her, she started babbling, so he hung up on her.

Rimzy blanked out. He didn't even bother going back in the

class to get Blue or his books. He just started running down the hall, and out of the building. He jumped in his whip and murked out.

As he entered the hospital, Rimzy walked past everybody on line at the receptionist desk. "Where is Saleena Brown?"

Normally, the receptionist would have told him to get on the line like everybody else, but she saw the worry in Rimzy's eyes and knew the terrible condition of the little girl.

She asked, "Are you a relative?"

"I'm her father."

"She's on the 5th floor in the Trauma Unit."

Without another word, Rimzy made his way to the elevators, all the while wondering who or what had put his baby girl in the Trauma Unit.

When he exited the elevators, he quickly proceeded to the nurse's desk and asked what room Saleena was in.

"Only family members are allowed on this unit."

"I AM HER FATHER!" he barked, with a forcefulness that was more out of worry than malice. The nurse realized the desperation in his voice for wanting to be with his daughter, and gave him directions to the room she was in.

The grief that came over Rimzy when he entered Room 518 would be unintelligible to anyone who never experienced the same scenario with their most precious possession. His internal pain alone was the equivalent of being smashed the ribs with a sledgehammer. He couldn't breathe.

When Sareena ran to him, he pushed her to the side, totally concentrating on his baby girl. She knew to give him space, and returned to her seat at the side of the bed.

Saleena's jaw was wired, both of her eyes were swollen shut, and her lips were puffy. Rimzy dropped to his knees at her bedside and hugged her unconscious little body.

"The doctors said she should be out for a little while because of the medications they had to give her during surgery," Sareena informed him.

"Surgery! What did you do to my baby? What did you do to my baby! I trusted you!"

Sareena was stuck, so Rimzy's mother stepped up and said, "Rimzy, Saleena was raped. She fought hard, but lost. Her jaw was broken, two of her ribs cracked, and she was sodomized. She had to undergo surgery to repair her ruptured anus."

They both broke down in tears and hugged each other, feeding strength from one another.

Thirty minutes later, Blue entered the room. When Rimzy didn't come back to class, he had started calling everywhere. It was Mama Bear who finally informed him that Saleena got hurt and Rimzy was at Jacobi. Blue, struck by his niece's condition, dropped to his knees the same as Rimzy.

Once Blue regained his composure, he said to Rimzy, "Give me the keys to your whip. I gave the tow truck driver a couple of pennies to hold up five minutes before towing your truck."

Forgetting he had parked right in front of the hospital doors, Rimzy fished in his pocket and handed Blue the keys.

After about two hours, Saleena came around and whispered in a very weary voice, "Daddy."

Rimzy put his head by her mouth. "I'm right here, baby. I'm right here."

"I did what you told me, Daddy. The police questioned me, but I told them I didn't know who did this to me because we handle our own business. Daddy, it was Flip. He hurt me, Daddy. You've got to hurt him back, Daddy."

Rimzy's mind was going a hundred miles an hour. *Flip. Flip? Flip!* He chanted the name in his head until a clear picture materialized. Flip was the guy hanging at Sareena's house the first night he went to visit them, when Sareenas glasses were broken.

"Don't worry about it, baby girl. You did good. Daddy is going to get him real good for doing this to you. Don't let anybody else know that you know who did this to you. The police will probably come by again tomorrow to question you. Believe me, I'm going to take care of him good. Okay?"

"Daddy, I'm tired. I'll talk to you later," she managed to say before passing out again.

Rimzy got up from her side and took a seat by the window. Nobody heard their exchange. His thoughts were measured and spaced out. They seemed to be coming in slow motion. After about ten minutes, Rimzy got up, looked at Sareena, and told her that they needed to talk. They left the room.

He and Sareena joined Blue, who was outside in the waiting area. Rimzy moved his eyes in the direction of the elevators, and without a word, Blue got up and walked with them to the elevators that took them to the ground level.

After Blue showed Rimzy where the truck was parked, they all got in, with Rimzy in the driver's seat, Sareena on the passenger's side, and Blue in the back seat. Rimzy was surprised at the calm tone he was able to muster up in order to address Sareena.

"Do you know who did this to my baby girl?"

"No."

"You've got no idea who could have done this?"

"I don't know, Rimzy." Sareena was scared to death, not knowing what Rimzy was capable of doing.

"Saleena told me who it was. It was your peoples Flip."

She started to say something, but Rimzy cut her off. "Now, I'm holding you responsible for what happened to my baby girl. If you didn't bring scrams around my baby's environment, this wouldn't have gone down."

"Listen. Calm down," Sareena, who was visibly shaken, managed to interject.

Rimzy ignored her and continued, "Even though I hold you responsible, I know for a fact you would never intentionally harm our child. So, what I'm going to do is take all the anger I've got for you at this moment and funnel it over to all the rage I have for him. This is what I need you to do. I need you to tell me everything you know about scrams. Where he hangs out, where he lives, who he hangs out with...everything."

By the time Rimzy left Sareena outside of the hospital, he and Blue didn't have much information on Flip. She had never gone to his house, and the only lead she could give them was that he scrambled on 118th Street between 7th and 8th. Rimzy instructed Sareena to stay at his mother's lab just in case Flip tried to retaliate. He then told her that he was going to give her some money to find a new lab, but in the meantime, for her not to give anyone Mama Bear's address or phone number. He also, forbade her to tell anybody they know who did it.

"Do not tell one person. I got this one. If by chance you do hear from scrams, tell him what happened to Saleena, but make sure you tell him that she couldn't remember who did this to her!" he said before pulling up in front of the hospital to drop Sareena off. Soon as she got out, Rimzy drove off to find a parking spot..

During the ride, Rimzy told Blue, "I got somebody up in Harlem that I'm going to get at tomorrow. You might as well go home for now. I'm getting ready to tell Ma to bounce. I'll holla at you tomorrow."

With that, they both got out of the truck and hugged tightly. When they finished their embrace, Blue looked at Rimzy and said,

"As soon as we catch him, not only are we gonna kill him, but we're gonna torture his ass."

Rimzy didn't say anything. Not only were they on the same page, but they were in the same paragraph. Flip was going to wish he was never born.

After Rimzy went upstairs and told his mother and Sareena that they should leave. Before she left, Rimzy told Sareena, "Get up here tomorrow morning."

* * * * * *

Rimzy stayed in the hospital all night and almost died when his daughter woke up screaming. Rimzy never had as much hatred for another human being in his life. He struggled to contain it as he hugged his baby girl.

First thing in the morning Rimzy made some calls and by the afternoon he had a phone number. Rimzy had met Rondu in Elmira. He had just come to the jail and was flagging the flaming set. Some Spanish kids tried to trap Rondu off in the gym. Peeping the move, Rimzy put Rondu on point. When the shit hit the fan, one out of the six dudes Rondu was with banged. The others scattered away from the drama like bitches. At that time, when the Spanish gang got one of their rival gang members trapped off, they would brand them, meaning they would write their initials on the rival's face with a single or double-edge razor.

Two dudes were holding Rondu down, while another got on top of him, getting ready to brand him. Rondu was thugged-out to the end. He spit on the kid who was going to cut him in the face and said, "Fuck you, bitch!"

Rimzy usually didn't get involved in gang dealings. He was what they called a neutral, meaning he wasn't in any gangs. He had a few men in different gangs, and dealt with each of them accordingly.

In any event, he didn't like any Spanish kids jumping no blacks, so he cut the kid that was going to cut Rondu and punched him. Before the kid fell, though, he cut Rimzy on his arm. Next, Rimzy tried to cut one of the kids that were holding Rondu down. That kid spun off of Rondu, and Rondu cut the other kid that was holding him down. Then Rondu popped up and ran to his man who was getting it on with two other kids. Rondu's man already had a decent cut on his face and was leaking badly. Rondu ran over and cut one of the kids from his eye straight down to his mouth. When the kid spun in an attempt to get away, Rondu's man cut part of his ear off. Now that the tables were turned, the Spanish kids scattered.

After it was all over, Rimzy ended up with thirty-eight stitches and got sent to the box for a year. While he was in the box, he got a boomerang from Rondu, which is a letter an inmate writes with a bogus address. When the letter came back "return to sender", the envelope would have the name of the inmate—in the upper left hand corner—that the other inmate wanted to contact. In the letter, Rondu told Rimzy that if it wasn't for him, his face would have been sick. Rondu told Rimzy he owed him big-time and gave Rimzy his mother's address and number. Rondu also told Rimzy that he felt bad that Rimzy got cut and got caught, while he got away.

The message came right on time, because Rimzy was in the box tight with himself for getting trapped in some gang dealings that didn't have anything to do with him. The scribe from Rondu acknowledging his sacrifice and recognizing that he saved his face made him smile. They met up in the Bullpens at a transit facility. Rondu was going to a minimum security facility, while Rimzy was going to Sing Sing. Rondu told Rimzy he would be home in six months and to get at him because he would never forget what Rimzy did for him. Rimzy never did get at Rondu, but he was going to get at him now because he needed information on Flip, and Rondu was just the person to give it to him.

At 6:00 p.m., Rimzy called Rondu's mom, who gave Rimzy Rondu's new number. After Rondu answered, Rimzy told him that he wanted to vibe with him, and once Rondu provided him with his address, Rimzy said he would be over in a black truck and then hung up.

By the time Rimzy got there, Rondu was standing in front of the building on 137th Street. Making small talk at first, they went through all of the formalities about what Rondu did once he got home. Rondu told Rimzy he lived with his girl, who was seven months pregnant, worked for UPS, and was basically trying to do right. When they met in Elmira, Rondu was eighteen and Rimzy was twenty three. They had both come a long way since then.

"Rondu, the last thing I'm trying to do is bust your bubble. I'm glad to see you're doing the right thing, but listen, I need you to do me a favor."

Rondu knew he was in the books big time with Rimzy and couldn't deny him anything. "Talk about it."

"Yo, you know this kid named Flip from 118th? He drives a black Pathfinder."

"Yea, I know Flip. That ain't his Path; that's his brother Flame's Path. Basically, that's his brother's block."

"Listen, I need to know any information you can discretely get about both of them, especially Flip. You still banging?"

"Not really. I grew up out of that. A lot of dudes aren't real and it's hard to decipher who's who. I throw it up, but I'm not in the frontlines like that. I keep it moving."

"The reason I asked is because I'm going to keep it fair. I'm trying to get at Flip, but I'm not trying to force your hand to set the trap."

"Listen, playboy, what you did for me goes beyond all that. I got crazy love for you. If all you want is info, that's no problem. As a matter of fact, if you want, I'll pop his head off."

"Nah, yo, the last thing I'm trying to do is put you out there like that. I got this. All I need is the info; that's it. Please don't blow the spot up. I don't want nobody to know I'm looking for him. Not even wifey on some pillow talk shit."

They looked at each other for a few seconds. Then Rondu said, "I got you."

Rimzy drove to Sammy's on City Island, where they ordered a big meal. After eating, Rimzy pushed an envelope over to Rondu with ten G's inside and told him it was for him and his new family. After Rondu stashed the paper in his pocket, Rimzy ordered two double shots of Henny. When it came, he made a toast, "to honor and love."

* * * * * *

Rimzy drove to the hospital after seeing Rondu and spent a couple of hours with his baby girl. When the doctors said they would release her in the morning, Rimzy told Saleena he would be there first thing to get her. After Saleena went to sleep, Rimzy handed Sareena ten G's and told her to go to a real estate broker to find another lab. Rimzy also told her that Saleena was coming to live with him.

"I'm sorry I let you and my baby down," she said as she lowered her head and started crying.

Rimzy grabbed her, held her, and said, "Don't be sorry; be careful."

As promised, Rimzy picked Saleena up from the hospital first thing in the morning and brought her home. He told her that she could stay downstairs with him, but he knew most of her time would be spent upstairs with his mother, her brother and cousins. When he opened the door to his mother's house, everyone yelled surprise. Everybody fussed over her, and she felt mad love in the house. Rimzy fell back and watched the family love, but inside, he was still fuming about the fact that someone had hurt his daughter. He couldn't even sleep.

The next week went by in a blur. Rimzy went to school at night, and spent time with his baby girl during the day, taking her to the movies, museums, and exhibits. On Thursday, while Rimzy was in school, his phone started vibrating; it was Rondu. After telling Blue he would be right back, he left the classroom and went to call Rondu back.

Once Rimzy connected with Rondu, they established that they would link up in two hours. Those two hours seemed like two years. Rimzy should have left because he definitely wasn't in class mode. When he pulled up to Rondu's lab, Rondu was in front of the building.

As they drove downtown, Rondu told him, "Nobody's seen Flip all week. It's like he vanished. His brother still be coming through, though. I don't know where he lives, but he fucks with this chick on 103rd Street, between 3rd and Lex. Here is the address, and I even got a picture of dude. That's all I got for now. I'll get back at you as soon as I get some more info. It's funny 'cause I ain't even have to ask them lame-ass cats nothing. They just talk for the sake of talking over there."

That night, Rimzy told Blue to rent a dark mini-van for the week. For three nights straight, Blue drove around downtown trying to spot Flip. On the fourth night, Blue caught up to Flip's brother

Flame.

After picking up Rimzy from his lab, Blue dressed in a pair of stockings, a skirt, a wig, and a pair of high-heel shoes, and then they quickly returned to the spot where Blue saw Flame's car parked. They waited three hours before Flame came out of one of his girl's buildings.

Rimzy slid the door open and got out of the van fixing his pants. Blue came out fixing his skirt. From Flame's perspective it looked like they had just finished fucking inside the van. Rimzy peeped Flame catch the whole throw off and laughed to himself. Rimzy had what looked like a beer bottle in a brown bag, and he was leaning on Blue like he was drunk. They were on a one-way street and Flames driver's door faced the sidewalk. After he hit the alarm and started to put the key in the door, Rimzy stumbled close to him while holding on to Blue and sticking his arm out to ask Flame if he wanted some beer.

Before Flame could respond, Rimzy stuck him with the stun gun and Flame immediately fell on the ground and started shaking. Rimzy opened the door and put Flame inside the driver's seat. Then he opened the back door and got in. By this time, Blue had gone back to the van, got in, and jetted.

From the back seat, Rimzy reclined the front seat all the way back, flipped Flame on his stomach, and dragged him to the back seat. Rimzy handcuffed Flame's arms behind his back, shackled his legs, and then wrapped one of his dog leashes around both sets of handcuffs, tying the leash into a tight knot. Rimzy then put some duct tape on Flame's mouth, jumped in the driver's seat, and slowly pulled off.

He drove down 3rd Avenue to 122nd, and then made a right. After picking up Blue who was waiting between 2nd and 1st, Rimzy climbed in the back, while Blue took over driving. They hit the Tri-

Borough Bridge to Queens. The reason why they went to Queens is so that if anybody saw them kidnap Flame, by the time they called the police, Rimzy and Blue would be in another jurisdiction.

Once they got over the bridge, Rimzy spoke to Flame. "I know you're probably wondering why we got you. Well, I want to ask you one question. And just to let you know, we're not playing any games."

Flame was face down on the floor with his arms in an uncomfortable position. Without warning, Rimzy took a hammer and started beating his elbows and hands. Flame's crying and screams of agony were muffled by the tape. He was hyperventilating and everything. When Rimzy turned him over, sheer panic could be seen in his eyes.

"Remember, I'm only going to ask you one time. Now are you ready for the question?"

Flame nodded his head furiously.

"Where is your baby-raping-ass brother?" Rimzy asked, and then snatched the tape off his mouth immediately so Flame wouldn't have time to think of a lie.

"He's on Staten Island," Flame replied.

"What's he doing out there?"

"He's lying up over there with one of his chicks."

Rimzy looked over to Blue. No words were exchanged, but Blue was on his way to the BQE, heading toward Shaolin.

"I don't know what your brother told you," Rimzy said, while placing the tape back over Flame's mouth, "but you've got nothing to do with this. Once we get him, you're free to go. All we want is his baby-raping ass."

All kinds of thoughts were going through Flame's head. *Baby-raping?* Flip had told Flame that he shot two kids and had to lay low for a few. At the time, Flame believed him, but now that he thought about it, one of their little cousins had accused Flip of some foul shit like that a couple of years ago. Flip swore up and down he didn't do it. That drama caused a lot of friction within the family. Since nobody could ever prove it, everybody dismissed it. She was a little fast-ass, but Flip was under investigation...and now this. Everything was coming to light. *Fuck Flip! Everything he gets, he deserves*, his brother rationalized.

A master at reading body language, Rimzy gave Flame all the time in the world to convince himself to give his brother up.

"Listen, this is how it's gonna go down. Once we get to S.I., you're going to call Flip and tell him to come downstairs and meet you. Do you have a problem with that?"

Flame shook his head no.

When they were on the Verrazano Bridge, Rimzy took the tape off and asked Flame, "Where at in Shaolin is he staying?"

"Killa hill."

Rimzy thought that was good, because it was right by the bridge. The last thing he wanted to do was get stopped by one of those nosey-ass racist Staten Island police because shit would get thick quick. No Surrender! No Retreat!

After they passed the tollbooth, Rimzy cut the dog leash and picked Flame up so he could give them the final directions to the girl's house. When they pulled in front, Rimzy jumped in the driver's seat and put on Flame's fisherman hat, while Blue got in the passenger's seat and passed Flame the phone.

Before Flame dialed the number, Blue told him, "Remember, you don't have nothing to do with this. If you want to live, you better play your cards right."

Flame told them he didn't know the number by heart, but it was in his phone. So, Blue fished in Flame's pocket, retrieved the phone, and handed it to Flame so that he could dial the number.

"Yo, I'm in front of your spot," Flame said into the receiver. "Come out. I got to holla at you, alright? Hurry up." After disconnecting the call, Flame told them, "He said he got to get dressed, but he'll be right out."

Five minutes later, Flip came out. As soon as Rimzy saw him, he wanted to jump out and beat fire out of him. Without even realizing it, he was gripping the steering wheel mad tight. Once Flip came down the steps, Blue got out and pointed towards the front seat, acting like he was getting in the backseat.

When Flip walked past Blue, the interior lights were turned off, so all he saw was Flame's fisherman hat. Before Flip could say anything or get inside, Blue struck him with the stun gun and pushed him into the front seat. Rimzy grabbed him while he was incapacitated and tried to straighten him up, while Blue got in the back passenger's door.

As soon as Blue shut the door, Rimzy pulled off. Blue reclined the passenger seat, dragged Flip in the back, positioned Flip's face by Flame's feet, and jimmy rigged him up just like his brother. At a light, Blue jumped in the driver's seat while Rimzy returned to the passenger's side.

Blue drove to Queens to a house the coalition was renovating. Blue pulled into the garage, shut the door, and they carried Flip into the house. Once inside, they got Flip settled in a chair set up on top of a lot of plastic. Then Rimzy went back into the garage, took Flame out, and put him in the trunk.

"Normally, I'm not the talkative type, but I've got to let you know something. You see how you gave your brother up? That's troubling. I mean, who's to say you won't get yourself caught up in a drug case, which is very likely because you're a drug dealer, and decide to give me up? Well, that's not something I'll have to worry about because I won't let you!"

With that, Rimzy reached into his waistband and pulled out a .380 and shot Flame three times in the head. Inside, Flip flinched when he heard the shots that came thundering from the garage.

Once back in the house, Rimzy went to the back and came out with an iron. He plugged it in, looked at Flip, and said, "Do you know you broke my daughter's jaw? She can't even eat regular food until the wires are removed from her mouth."

As he talked, he pulled out a brand new stainless steel rug cutter, grabbed his shirt real hard and started cutting from the top of his right chest across to his lower left stomach. Rimzy literally cut him out of his shirt. When he had him butt-ass naked, he had an outburst. "You raped my baby!"

With that said, Rimzy and Blue started beating Flip's ass. Rimzy made sure he broke his jaw. After they beat him unconscious, they positioned him upright in the chair. A short while later he regained consciousness. By then, the iron was steaming hot. Rimzy picked it up and placed it hard against Flip's chest, while Flip's cries were muffled by the tape over his mouth. When Rimzy tried to pull it off, he had to yank two times, and when it did detach from the skin, it came off with a nasty sticking sound, with skin left on the iron's plate. Next, he pressed the iron on Flip's leg. By now, mucus was running out of Flip's nose, as he continued to scream against the duct tape.

Rimzy wanted to take it off and hear him scream. Flip had even pissed on himself. This time, they had him standing up and bending over the back of the chair. They had to wake him up again because he passed out from the pain that was too much for him to bear.

Rimzy went to the back and returned with a bottle in a brown bag and a small propane tank. When he took the bag off, there was a rat in the bottle. Rimzy had paid Dog-man to put the rat in the bottle and make a special metal top so the rat couldn't bust out.

Rimzy showed Flip the rat and told him, "You know, a rat has no bones. Well, I want to test that myself."

While Blue held him still, Rimzy went around Flip, took the top off the bottle, spread his ass cheeks, and stuck the opening of the bottle up his ass. Right after that, Rimzy lit the propane tank's nozzle. With a short burst, the tank ignited, and Rimzy turned the knob so the flame grew larger. In one quick movement, the fire was on the bottle. The rat started running around the bottle faster and faster before bolting to the top, right into Flip's ass. Flip started moving around, but most of his energy was spent.

Rimzy and Blue then carried Flip, with the bottle still stuck up his ass and the rat nowhere in sight, to the trunk. Once he was situated, they went and got two gallon jugs of gasoline and another bottle out the back, placing them in the back seat. They left the propane tanks behind.

They poured some bleach on the floor and scrubbed the whole area where they had tortured Flip even though they didn't see any blood. After they finished scrubbing it with the bleach, they mopped the floor, dumped the water down the toilet, and flushed it a few times. Then they placed the mops, scrub brushes, and jugs in the trunk as well. Sweating like crazy from all their work, they looked around and everything was in order.

It was 4:30 a.m. by the time they backed out of the garage. Rimzy went back over the Tri-borough, got off at 125th, let Blue out on 2nd Avenue, and kept it moving. He drove to Park Avenue and 118th Street, jumped in the back seat, removed the plastic from the bodies, and started pouring gasoline on them.

Rimzy poked Flip with the mop handle, and his body moved. "Wake up. I wouldn't want you to miss the grand finale."

Rimzy finished dousing everything with gas, then opened the back door and walked around the truck with the bottle. Once he got to the back door, he emptied the rest of the bottle on the back seat, and it dripped down to a puddle on the floor. Rimzy quickly took out the other two gallon jugs and poured them over the exterior of Flame's jeep. With that done, he ran to the end of the gas trail, lit it, and started running toward Madison Avenue.

Rimzy was three-quarters down the block, when he heard the explosion. He looked back at the inferno he caused and thought, *Damn, I might have overdone it with the gas.*

When Rimzy turned the corner, Blue was right there waiting. He jumped in the van and they drove down Madison Avenue to the 3rd Avenue Bridge, which took them to the Bronx.

On the drive to Blue's lab, Rimzy and Blue didn't talk. When they got to the projects, about a mile from Blue's building, Rimzy reached over, released the holster containing the Desert Eagle, and passed it to Blue. Rimzy then grabbed the brown bag with the .380. Blue had already broken the gun into four pieces. Rimzy gave Blue some dap and exited the van.

After that, Rimzy went to four different buildings and dropped a piece of the gun in each incinerator. Then he walked around the corner, jumped in his whip, and drove to the house.

* * * * * *

The next couple of weeks went by in slow motion. The paper ran a small article about the bodies, and they speculated it was a drug-related crime. Rimzy knew the cops had Flame labeled as a drug dealer because of his previous arrest on alleged drug charges. Once homicide looked at his file, they would automatically assume that, and that would stop them from putting their all into the investigation. He would be labeled as just another black drug dealer killed. It wasn't like he was a prominent member of the community or the son of a rich person, so they saw it as no major loss.

Chapter 23

With the knock of the judge's hammer, Ramel was a free man. The fam threw a welcome home party at club Body the next day, which was followed by a nighttime celebration for the friends.

As they sat at the bar awaiting a round of drinks Rimzy and Ramel engaged in light conversation; the kind that Rimzy had missed during the long years that Ramel was away. "I know you got all of them car books I sent you, so tell me which one you want," said Rimzy. Ramel replied, "Damn, you doing the thing like that?" Ramel then jokingly put on the most sophisticated voice he could conjure and said, "well my intense research has yielded me to conclude that the current automobile of choice is the BMW M6 hard top, because I don't feel like dropping the top as of yet." Rimzy had to laugh, but was impressed with his brother's vehicle selection.

"That M has that techtronic transmission. I like your style. What color?" he asked.

"Most likely gangster black."

"Ok, Ok. It feels good having you home. The Fam has got a lot going on, but I don't want to stress you. Just know that everything we do now is legitimate. I don't want you out here making us hot with your bull shit. Anyway, I'm not going to preach to you too long. Just stay up and stay home. Statistics state that the highest recidivism rate occurs within the first 90 days. Those are some mean stats, so stay sharp out here."

Lil' bro couldn't get in a word, but was paying close attention to his big brothers words of wisdom. It was unfortunate that lil' bro picked up a bad coke habit in jail, a Mexican kid that was in the cell right next to him was getting it majorly and had no problem giving Ramel more than his share. After a couple of months he was good and hooked. Ramel worried that Rimzy would pick up on his habit, but he vowed to put an end to it as soon as he could.

They stayed up into the wee hours of the morning laughing, reminiscing and making plans for the future. Rimzy found himself constantly repeating "Its good to have you home." He filled Ramel in on various ventures that the family had taken on in his absence. "You know Black and Blue got that club, don't go crazy in there, because most of females are going to be cheesing all in your face. You got a good thing at home so, stay focused." Ramel soaked up all of the knowledge that Rimzy had to give. He continued, "You should go to the engineering school, so you could learn to make some beats. That is just a suggestion. I remember how you use to play them hard beats and you use to somehow know when a song was a hit before the radio started blowing it up. That is another thought, you could A&R for the label we started. You got an ear for music. Use it." Lil bro was definitely feeling his brother's vibe. He just had some issues he had to resolve. He heard that Mike Jones—the rat bastard who testified at his trial—was also home. First and foremost he wanted to get that monkey off his back.

That coke had him up every night straight for two weeks waiting on the roof for Mike Jones. He finally caught up to him one night at 4 in the morning. He did not say a word, when Jones stepped off the elevator he got the surprise of a lifetime. He froze up as lil bro walked right up on him, face to face, and mushed him in the face real hard. It was so intense that it sent him flying backwards. By the time he recovered lil bro had the silencer equipped Glock 10 aimed at his face. Mike Jones took a deep breath like he either was going to scream or maybe yell NO, although no sound made it out of his mouth, because lilbro let him have it. When he finished, Ramel leaned over him and put 10 ounces of crack cocaine in the witness pocket in order to put a whole other spin on the homicide investigation, preventing anyone from zeroing in on him.

Satisfied that he had closed one final chapter from his past, Ramel decided that from that point, he was only moving forward. The coke that he placed on Mike Jones was the last that he would ever touch.

Chapter 24

Rimzy sat back and thought about all the things in his life that reflected his ways and actions. There were three things that his life revolved around: his family, his development, and his future.

Rimzy's mother was the foundation of his existence, so he brought her a plaza, which housed a fast food restaurant named Mama's, where a person could order a dollar beef patty or a bucket of fried jumbo shrimp. Next to Mama's was a liquor store, then a barber and beauty shop, a 24 hour laundry/ dry cleaners, a clothing store, and on the end was an 99cent store. Across from the stores was a double-sided thirty-car parking lot.

The plaza was rebuilt from the remains of a gas station and the huge abandoned parking lot that sat just next door. Mama Bear's real estate friend helped secure the deal, but it was Rimzy who noticed the property sitting dead smack in the middle of the hood. Rimzy and an architect drew up the blueprints, with the architect maximizing the property Rimzy had purchased and putting Rimzy's idea to paper with actual dimensions.

Once the blueprints were in hand, the next person Rimzy utilized was the collisions analyst, who changed all of the blueprints into mathematical equations. The analyst was a young black man who broke the cost of everything down. The way he broke things down really impressed Rimzy, who admired his professionalism.

After Rimzy had the figures for the entire inventory, he had to figure out how much the labor would cost. Rimzy had a team put together from his coalition connections. Without disturbing the normal day-to-day operations of the coalition, Rimzy handpicked the personnel, who took various trades, including carpentry, floor covering, electrical, plumbing, and masonry.

The next stage of Rimzy's plan was to get a demolition crew to tear down the old gas station and dispose of the scraps. Rimzy started his own construction company, and with his own tax number, it was official.

Rimzy cut corners on the demolition cost by renting a minibus, filling it with Mexicans, and bringing them to the work site where he had two foremen waiting. When Rimzy worked for Shabazz's construction firm he gained a whole new respect for Mexican workers. They did things that Rimzy and the other workers could handle. For that reason Rimzy looked out for them first when hiring for his own company. The foremen divided the Mexicans into teams to do various projects, and it took less than a week for the Mexicans to break down the structure, get rid of the scraps, and dig a hole to set the foundation.

It took a month for the project to be completed. Even though Rimzy had two foremen making sure the operation ran smoothly, he still made spot checks. He personally oversaw the project from beginning to end.

Rimzy paid all of his workers handsomely, and at the end of the job he gave everyone a big bonus. He had all of their information and was in negotiations to buy another piece of property, where he was planning to construct a building. When they completed the job, he put a bug in everyone's ear about the new project, so they could expect more work in the future.

Once all of the plaza's cosmetics were completed, Rimzy had a top-of-the-line security system installed. He wanted a camera inside and outside of each store, and all of the cameras were set up to a central computer so he or his mother could monitor the stores from their homes or laptops. Rimzy had a sophisticated system. Not only could he see from the cameras, but he could hear what was going on in the stores, as well.

In the back of the clothing store, Rimzy had an office built for his mother. The way Rimzy set things up each store ran independently with its own manager. All Rimzy's mother had to do was watch over the managers and make sure everything ran smoothly.

The managers took inventory every week to make sure no stock was missing. Still, he knew that no matter what he did he would always take losses, which he planned to keep at a bare minimum.

Everything scanned on the register was checked off on the inventory list, so it wasn't hard for Rimzy or his mother to check the computer and see what items needed to be re-ordered. Rimzy's mother was the only one who could place orders, so all of the managers had to go through her. Rimzy periodically conducted spot checks to make sure the figures matched the computer.

Rimzy understood the laws of business, and hired nothing but dime pieces in his mother's establishments. Business started off slow, but gradually picked up as the months passed.

After about five months of the business doing well, two Russian men with very serious faces entered the clothing store. They were dressed immaculately in their suits, but it was obvious that they were not really businessmen. They had that edge about them, and the black Mercedes Benz they pulled up in only enhanced their facade.

They entered the clothing store on some smooth shit, and one of them asked, "Can we speak to the owner of this fine establishment?"

The manager of the clothing store explained that the owner was not in. About a month later, as Mama Bear was getting out of her 750 BMW, the same two Russian men followed behind her.

Before she knew what was happening, they ushered her into her office.

"Listen, Mrs. Brown, we know you are the sole owner of these fine establishments. I'll get straight to the point. What my associates and I want to do is guarantee that no unforeseen misunderstandings occur. Basically, we're offering you our security services for a year. We would like $10,000 as an initial payment, and then we will require $2,000 a month. Now, Mrs. Jones, we're respectable businessmen. We hope you'll see that it would be a wise decision to use our firm, but the choice is yours. We will be back in one week for your response to our proposition."

Rimzy had a scowl on his face as he watched the videotape. He had to admit, they were very professional shakedown artist. If the tape was brought to the police, there wouldn't be enough evidence to build a case and he knew the repercussions would be deadly. Telling was not an option in Rimzy's book. He was well acquainted with the codes of the streets, though things on the street were on another level versus prison. In prison, telling is the norm, but real G's didn't tell no matter what.

Rimzy's mind was moving one-hundred miles an hour. His first plan of action was to get Mama Bear as far away from the drama as possible.

Rimzy was tight. "I can't even set my own mother out with a business without some fake-ass gangsters pressing issues."

Rimzy had no illusions about the Russian mob. They were some ruthless, over-the-top, murder-your-whole-family type of gangsters. Rimzy knew he had to figure out how to handle the situation very delicately.

The two gangsters pressed the buzzer to the office and Rimzy buzzed them in. If they were surprised to see him sitting there, they didn't show it in the least. Rimzy was dressed to fit the role he was playing. He had on blue slacks, a pair of brown loafers, and a blue and brown striped button-down shirt. He put a borderline nervous look on his face. He didn't want to overdo it.

"Hello, gentlemen. Can I help you with anything?"

They looked at each other for a split second, before the shorter one said, "We're here to see Mrs. Brown the owner."

Rimzy responded, "I'm her son, and in a position to handle her affairs."

They looked at one another again for a split second, which is all it took for Rimzy to speculate it would only be a matter of time before he would be able to exploit these two birds.

Again, the short one spoke. "Did she tell you about our arrangement?"

Rimzy shook his head yes.

"Do you have the payment for the services we're going to provide for you?" the short one asked.

"I sure do," Rimzy responded. He wasn't wasting any words. As he said that, he reached into the desk drawer and attempted to pass the envelope to the short one, but the tall one snatched it out of his hand.

Rimzy made a mental note: very rude. *He will pay for that; both of them will pay.*

After the tall one finished thumbing through the money, he put it inside his jacket pocket and told Rimzy, "We'll be back next month on the same day. If you have any problems…"

While talking, he fished around in his pocket and retrieved a card. "Take this card, and call if there is ever a problem."

He suddenly slammed the card on the desk, leaving one finger on it for a few seconds for effect. Rimzy jumped at the loud smacking sound made by the force, but only to feed into the visual effect he knew the goons were looking for.

Rimzy was far from scared or nervous. As a matter of fact, he was laughing like crazy inside at their fake thug antics. They would never know Rimzy's true intentions. Rimzy was a master of his emotions.

Rimzy saw the smirk on the jokers' faces when he jumped. *Damn, I'm good,* he thought, as they swaggered toward the door like they owned the place.

Rimzy had half a mind to hit the automatic lock, pull out the Desert Eagle equipped with silencer that was suctioned to the under casing of his desk, and have his way with them. Instead, he watched them walk out to their car and leave.

Little did they know, Blue had put a top-of-the-line listening and tracking device under their car, and was now following five blocks in back of them in a black Ford Taurus, listening and recording their conversation.

Rimzy had done his homework, even on the smallest details. Rimzy found out through demographics online that the black Ford Taurus was the most registered vehicle in New York, which meant it was the most likely car to be seen on the road. Therefore, Blue was almost invisible.

After a month of listening and watching, Rimzy felt he knew enough about them to plan his counter action.

Rimzy called a meeting at the lab he bought his mother. Rimzy kept the basement for times as such. The basement was scarcely furnished. There was a queen-size bed in the bedroom. No dresser or anything else in the room except for the safe that was bolted to the closet floor. The living room contained nothing but bookshelves filled with educational books.

The dining room had a big, black, round table with tall back chairs. The only other thing in the dining room was a picture of seven black men with big guns in their hands. They had on black suits with black hats, and each one had a hand stacked in the center on top of another. Their other hands were pointed in the air. The only parts that were illuminated were their hands in the circle and the big guns in the air. Nobody could make out the men's faces. All you could see was a couple of eyes in the shadows. On the bottom of the picture were the words "CODE OF THE STREETS." The picture was straight gangster.

Rimzy looked around the table at his four cohorts. Blue, Black, his brother Ramel and his cousin Rasheeda all met his stare and were acknowledged by a slight head nod. He trusted all four people at the table whole-heartedly.

Rimzy set the meeting off by saying, "I've come to understand that these so-called extortionists have a weak organization. They don't have half the discipline or structure we have." They went on discussing the make-up, hierarchy and function of the Russian Mafia.

After the meeting, they all decided to race out to City Island to get something to eat. Once there, they popped a bottle of Cristal, and Rasheeda made a toast.

"May we be successful in all of our ventures to come."

After everybody touched glasses, nobody made a sound for about two minutes. Everybody was in their own world, looking at their menus and thinking about what they were going to order. They all ordered an assortment of seafood, fried red snapper being the favorite. Ramel was the only one that ordered the mushroom steak, well-done, with a baked potato.

"You're the only person I know that comes to City Island and orders steak," Rimzy said. "If we go to the steak house, what are you going to order, Italian?"

Ramel replied, "I'll order whatever the fuck I want to order, wherever and whenever!"

"Such hostility. Where do you think you're at, the center yard? If you were somebody else, I could take that tone and use of profanity as disrespect, leading me to have to put my ice pick in you. Lucky for all of us, we are not in the yard and you are my only biological brother left on the planet. I love you to death, so I'll laugh, drink expensive champagne, and talk shit right along with you."

"Boy, you have a way with words. I just have a taste for a well-done steak smothered in mushrooms. And, I love you, too."

Ramel had just come home and he still had that rah rah in his system. Rimzy hoped he would snap out of that jail mentality, so he checked him in a subtle way that would have went over the head of the common listener.

They talked shit, ate their food, talked a little business, and then kept it moving to the parking lot where they continued talking. Fifteen minutes later, they were rounding the circle that led in a host of various directions, everyone branching off into their own zone.

Chapter 25

The jokers knew the tables had turned against them as soon as they entered the office. The office lights were brightly lit and they saw Rimzy seated behind his desk in a black hooded sweat suit. By the time they registered that Rimzy's attire was out of character, they were pushed real hard from the back and rammed into a piece of Plexiglas.

It felt like they were being beaten with Louisville Sluggers, but in actuality, Rimzy and his family had rigged one hundred bricks in a reinforced net over the door. When they bounced off the glass, Rimzy pulled a string, which released the bricks and literally broke them down. They were on the floor with their arms and legs in awkward, abnormal positions. While the bricks were falling, Rimzy laughed. He started off chuckling, but the chuckles turned into uncontrollable laughter, laughter that brought him to his knees with his hands banging on the floor.

Blue came in the office, looked at Rimzy on the floor, and had an urge to laugh, but the issue at hand was far too serious. It took Rimzy a few moments to regain his composure, but he walked over to the mangled bodies and quoted Biggie: "So you want to be hardcore?" Then he flipped it to Scarface: "Look at you now." Then it was all him: "You feeling fucked up right now?"

He squatted next to the two men in an official hood stance, and said, "I'm a firm believer in the kinetic laws. One in particular at this precise moment, and I'm going to quote it to you: 'What goes around comes around'. Believe me, it has come full circle right in your face. Your punk asses are in a world of trouble."

Rimzy placed his face closer to theirs. "You fake-ass gangsters can't be serious. You don't even know who the original gangsters are. How could you try to shake us down? We're unshakeable. I was just waiting for the right time to bust your motherfuckin' heads wide open!"

Blood was flowing down both of their faces. One of them had a mean gash from his temple to the middle of his cheek.

"Now, you guys are going to give me the password to the vault. And just to let you know that I'm dead serious about getting information from you…"

Ramel came out, as if on cue, with a big sledgehammer and started slamming it into the bricks with full force. Both men started screaming in agony.

"Okay!" the bigger man screamed. "I'll tell you everything you want to know."

Big man folded up like a beach chair. The little one was semi-conscious, babbling nothingness. It wasn't hard to tell that they had all of the fight knocked out of them. Their survival skills kicked in full throttle. Basically, they were willing to do anything to walk out of the office on their own. They knew their chances were next to nil, but no one wants to concede to their demise. They were in survival mode for real.

"You don't even do homework on the people you try to extort," Rimzy said. "If you did, you would have known that my mother had three sons. One son got murdered in cold blood. The youngest got convicted for murdering the oldest brother's murderer. His conviction was later overturned because witnesses changed their stories. And, if you dug deeper, you would have known that one of the witnesses got murdered something gruesome. I think he got two face shots. How about the fact that the middle son, who is me by the way, did seven years in prison for killing his mother's abusive lover? Couldn't you put the pieces of the puzzle together? Well, bitches, the shoe is definitely on the other foot now, so what you gonna do? What you gonna do?"

The two men wallowed in their defeat and Rimzy continued to preside over them triumphantly.

"How the fuck did you think you could wrap your fat little fingers around my neck? Come to find out, a little late you might say, your fingers aren't nearly long enough to fuck with the truth. That is what we are to you, you fuckin' bitch...the truth. The truth shall weed out the phonies. So consider yourselves weeds, and right now, you're getting pulled from the earth. Well, I guess I've taken up too much of your time."

With his sermon done, Rimzy spun around on some Michel Jackson shit, knelt down by both of their faces, and smacked each of them five times. After that, he left the room smiling.

As soon as Rimzy left, Black and Ramel started picking up the bricks very delicately.

"Boy, you two are lucky. Usually, he doesn't let people who cross his family live," Black said.

After they cleared the bricks off the crumbled up bodies, they moved the men over to a big piece of black plastic. Before the two goons could understand what was going on, it was too late. Black and Ramel came running at them with aluminum bats and beat them to death.

* * * * * *

The morning sky looked extra shinny as it glistened off of the East River. The morning started out slow. At 9:00 a.m., the leader of the Russian mob was murdered. Rimzy's plan used one of the oldest war tactics: Divide and Conquer. Rimzy knew they had five underbosses and two sons who were all thirsty for power.

Rimzy came up with an official plan. First things first, he planned to murder the head of the Russian mob and let things fall as they may.

The leader of the Russian mob was about to eat lunch at his favorite eatery in SoHo. It was a small mom-and-pop Russian spot. The Boss was a short, frail man. He wore a Blue Armani suit, wing-tip shoes, and a fedora hat.

They were semi-organized. First, a car pulled up before his arrival with two armed men who observed the inside of the restaurant, as well as the block it was situated on. After they thought they secured the area, a black Cadillac limo came around the corner, and two bigger, brawny henchmen popped out. The two that arrived earlier were strategically positioned on each side of the entrance to the establishment, while the other two got into position. However, before that could happen, the head came rushing out of the limo talking shit.

"Enough with the shenanigans. I'm starving. Besides, didn't you guys see all of the gangster movies? They always kill the boss while he's eating. That is where you focus…"

Before he could complete the rest of his sentence, he and his constituents were bombarded with a mirage of bullets from two strategically placed rooftop assassins. There were no shots heard, which made the situation more eerie. The boss' first reaction was that one of his henchmen punched him in the side of his head because he felt a hard smack as he watched his hat fly.

He started to realize what was happening as he felt an even harder smack, which spun him around and sent him flying backward. As he flew, he saw his so-called security doing an awkward dance. It all happened so fast, his mind didn't have time to register any real conclusions before everything went black.

When it was all said and done, he died in the gutter with an empty stomach, not knowing that there was a big difference between gangster movies and reality. As for the rest of his crew, after they finished doing their dance, they fell harder than a sack of potatoes, and they weren't from Idaho.

After Rimzy and Blue emptied their one-hundred round clips, they calmly put their fully-automatic machine guns in matching black duffle bags, ran to the roofs doors, and hit the steps that led to the back doors. Ramel was waiting when Rimzy came out of the back door, and from there, they drove around the corner and picked up Blue. By the time everyone came out from cover and called the police, Rimzy's three-man team were whipping up the FDR, burning uptown.

* * * * * *

Within an hour, the remaining members of the Russian mob called an emergency meeting at their Brighton Beach location; one of three that Rimzy had staked out in preparation for the plan. After another hour and a half, a lot of faces that Rimzy had thumb tacked to the planning board at his honeycomb hideout had gathered. Everyone except one of the underbosses—who they already found out was in a bad car accident—arrived, and the meeting started.

The oldest son started things off. "I want the heads of the people responsible for my father's death on my table within twenty-four hours…"

That was all he got out before the C-4 Blue put on the back wall exploded into a ball of fire. There was complete panic by those who weren't fatally wounded by the blast. They started running toward the front of the building, where they were chopped down by one-hundred round clips from two MAC-11's.

After the first few bodies fell, the rest stopped and tried to get organized. While they were plotting on how to get out of the building, Rimzy and Blue threw six grenades in rapid succession. The sound of the grenades going off was some Vietnam shit...straight brutal.

By the time the missing underboss got out of the hospital, all of the other mob bosses were up in smoke. Everybody was in cahoots about what happened. Being that he was the only underboss alive, all power transferred to him. He was in high demand, with everybody trying to get in contact with him.

He put everybody on hold that night in order to get his thoughts together. He scheduled a meeting for the following morning. As soon as he entered his house, he went straight to the bar and fixed a triple shot of vodka. After two of those, he took a shower, and got into bed.

While lying there, he started talking to himself, "I must have a concussion."

That thought was immediately put to rest when he heard Rimzy, who was sitting in a chair in the corner of the room.

"So the chosen one has finally come home?"

The underboss sat up, trying to focus in on the voice, but all he could see was a shadowy form. The one thing he had no problem seeing, though, were the two Desert Eagles held crisscrossed on a lap.

"I'm going to make this short and sweet," Rimzy told him.

Chapter 26

Mama Bear's real estate connect put Rimzy on to some property that a decease ninety year old left to the state. It was right along the lines of what Rimzy was looking for.

The realtor showed Rimzy in black and white that in the three month period during which the property was on the market, the offering price had already been lowered twice. Rimzy quickly acquired the four-acre property in Riverdale which, at its peak, valued at 2.5 million dollars. Because the previous owner did not have the resources to maintain the property, the overgrowth had diminished its value.

Rimzy wasn't trying to live in anybody's great, great grandkid's house. He was planning to tear down the mansion that sat in the middle of the property with its long windy roadway. If he could have salvaged the mansion, Rimzy would have built two houses on each side of the roadway and still had a little space to play with before the windy road stopped in front of the mansion.

There were two things that really had Rimzy open about the property. The first was that it sat up high. For some reason, Rimzy wanted to look down on things. It symbolized that he was on top. Secondly, was the property was surrounded by a twenty-foot granite wall.

Rimzy already had the blueprints made up before he even acquired the land. Rimzy was building his own community. He was going to build six mini-mansions and a big recreation center, with a gymnasium and swimming pool. Rimzy wanted the outside equipped with two of the biggest play centers on the market. He also intended to place an in-ground swimming pool next to the barbeque and lounge area off to the side.

Rimzy picked six foremen, one to supervise each house. He let the foremen pick their own crews to do the basic labor. Through word of mouth, Rimzy found out about a construction company that was going out of business and about to have all of its assets liquidated. Rimzy stepped to the business, and was cut and dry when he dealt with the group of children who mishandled their deceased father's business.

"Listen, you could have the government liquidate your company and get nothing out of the deal, or you could sign over all your debts to me and still come out with a little change in your pockets to help you get started in another kind of venture."

When it was all said and done, Rimzy had an office and an arsenal of trucks and machinery. Rimzy worked out an agreement with the bank whereby he paid the minimum down on a loan that bailed the company out of debt. He paid the owners a nice amount and still had some left over for the refurbishing of some of the trucks and other equipment that was neglected. As it stood, the paperwork wasn't complete, but Rimzy somehow got to use the equipment he needed to clear and dig up the property so they could put the foundations down.

Rimzy made it his business to be there early the day the cement trucks were coming. He watched and learned everything from the foremen. He wanted to be there to see the process in action. He wasn't actually getting his hands dirty, but he was going to know how to build every step of the way.

It took three months for everything to be done, and Rimzy had spent a pretty penny on his security. Some people would think Rimzy was paranoid, but Rimzy called it peace of mind.

All of the mini-mansions were built with the same floor plan. They weren't castles, but they were a far cry from the PJ's. The houses were brick and each had a driveway leading to a two-car garage.

There was a little walkway that led to a couple of steps. After the steps, each had a little porch area with two pillars on each side. Once the door was open, you entered a rotunda. The rotunda led to the sunken living room with one of three fireplaces. When you walked to the left, you reached the stairway that went up to the second floor, which had a wrap around hallway that allowed people to look down into the living room.

If you walked to the right after the rotunda, you would be able to walk all the way around the living room in an elevated hallway that ended at the kitchen. There were a few doors in-between the rotunda and the kitchen. The master bedroom took half of the second floor, and the master bathroom and walk-in closet took half of that.

The family had their chests poked out the day of the move. On that day they really could say that they took it to the next level. The houses were distributed as such: Momma Bear, Rimzy, Blue, Black, Ramel and his family, and Rimzy's cousin Rasheeda.

It took a few weeks for everybody to paint and furnish their houses with their individual flair. When it was all done, everybody's lab was decked out with top-of-the-line appliances, electronics, and furniture.

Chapter 27

Rimzy had video cameras strategically placed in all of the houses. Each house had its own set up for privacy, but he had his set up so he could watch his house and his mother's. He had hidden cameras all over the place.

One day, he was in is office checking his e-mail, when he glanced at the screen above his computer, feeding live video from the security camera in one of the children's rooms, and saw Saleena giving what seemed to be a sermon. Rimzy didn't have cameras in the children's rooms for spying, but rather for security reasons. Nevertheless, he hit the sound button to see what she was talking about, and boy, was he shocked to hear what his daughter was talking about. He couldn't understand where the venom was coming from.

"Y'all little motherfuckers better respect me. Fuck all of them other motherfuckers. I'm the head motherfucker in charge in this motherfuckin' house, and if any of you motherfuckers want to challenge me, speak now or forever hold your peace."

She looked around the circle with an ice grill, but nobody was ready to go against the grain.

"Good, I thought you would see things my way. Now I have a list of…"

Before she could finish, she was wiped off her royal heiress ass by her neck and walked out of the room with her feet dangling in the air. Rimzy snatched her up without breaking his stride or saying a word.

The children were speechless for at least a minute before Jamal spoke. "I guess her smooth-talking, slick-walking ass got shut down."

They all yelled in unison, "Shut 'em down, shut 'em, shut 'em down." It was an old school Public Enemy song they shouldn't have known about, but Rimzy loved some old school rap, so the children knew a lot of old school tunes. After their little chorus, they all fell out laughing.

Danté added, "Did you see the look on her face? Her eyes got so wide I thought they were going to pop out of her head." He opened his eyes wide to demonstrate and accentuate his joke.

Soon, they were all walking around holding their necks with their eyes open wide. They laughed so hard their stomachs started hurting. Little did they realize they would not see their cousin again for a minute.

Rimzy carried Saleena by her neck straight out of the house to the car, and they headed to the hood.

"So you think you're better than everybody else? You think the fam couldn't survive without you? Who the hell do you think you are, the almighty, anointed, omnipotent, all-knowing one? Baby girl, you have a lot to learn in this world, but let me drop a jewel on you. The more you know, the less you realize you know. Now, I'm going to give you some time to reflect on your values and what is important to you. You are the oldest and I want you to be a role model, not some dictator imposing unfair selfish polices on your younger siblings."

Rimzy drove her to their old house.. Sareena knew the house, but not the basement, which was fully furnished and a comfortable spot to live in. Rimzy took the phone cord and TV cord so Saleena wouldn't have any distractions. He also took all the knives and sharp objects, just in case she tried to get any bright ideas.

"I'm going to leave you here indefinitely so you can get your thoughts together, and realize who is who and what is what. I want a written report when I come for you, telling how much you miss everybody and what qualities you miss the most about each person."

He pulled a pen and pad out of a drawer and placed it in front of her. With that said, he left her to be alone with her thoughts. Rimzy didn't believe in beatings. He believed Saleena would learn a whole lot more sitting in the basement for a week alone.

Rimzy felt that most people got so caught up in society's norms that they failed to realize the finer things in life. So, he wanted to give her some time to get to know herself. He wanted the layers of character to be peeled away like the skin of an onion. Hopefully, as she went deeper into the core, she would come to realize she didn't like what she found. Rimzy learned this technique from his incarceration. He spent many months in the box, totally isolated from everyone.

The honeycomb was nowhere near as cruel as the box. If he locked her in the bathroom, cut off the water, and starved her, it would be more comparable. Rimzy wasn't trying to take it that far; he was just using the concept.

It hurt Rimzy to leave his only daughter alone, but her attitude toward the fam had to change. With her being the oldest, it would be too easy for the other children to fall victim to her way of thought. Children are very impressionable and Rimzy didn't want any negative influences around them.

After Rimzy left, Saleena sat around in a daze. She couldn't understand how one day she was queen, calling mad shots, and the next day, it was all taken away. She went through a lot of channels before she clicked to the right one.

First, she went through the denial stage. She blamed everybody but herself for her problems. Next, she went through the self-pity stage where she felt everyone should be sorry for her. It took her two days before she even thought about herself as being the master of ceremony in her situation. After she started to get a grip on her emotions, she started to scout out her surroundings besides the kitchen, where she had enough microwavable TV dinners and juices to feed an army. After a brief intake of observation, Saleena's eyes rested on a set of strategically placed books.

Rimzy was ecstatic when he saw her pick out "Stolen Legacy". He and his mother had been watching her every move through hidden cameras since she got there. Rimzy saw a lot of people try to hang themselves in the box in prison because they couldn't deal with themselves, and he definitely wasn't trying to have his plan backfire.

By the time Rimzy came to get Saleena after seven days, she had rebuilt herself into a bigger, stronger child. He didn't want to brake her spirits, but he had to give her enough time to get pass the rebellious stage. As soon as Rimzy entered the basement, he was greeted with warm spirits.

"Hey, Daddy. Listen, I've had a lot of time to think and I've come to realize that I owe you and the entire fam an apology for the way I've been acting. All we got is us; everything else is secondary. From now on, I'm going to be a positive developmental part of my little cousins' and brothers' lives. I'm going to make my contribution to shaping and molding them into the stars they're going to be. Now I see their potential is unlimited."

Rimzy looked at her and didn't say a word. He knew his technique was on point, but the feedback he got was over the top. Rimzy was feeling himself and he knew that could be a weakness. He dropped down to one knee, looked into her eyes, which he believed was the doorway to the soul, and verified that the truth was coming out of her mouth. No words were spoken by Rimzy. He just grabbed her up and hugged her for a few minutes.

When they pulled into the driveway, there were no cars and all the house lights were off. The look of disappointment was clearly visible on Saleena's face.

Rimzy hit on her nerve by telling her, "Everybody went on a cruise. They'll be back next week."

As they walked into a dark house, Sareena was getting ready to ask her father a question, when the lights cut on and the whole fam was there.

"SURPRISE!"

Overwhelmed by the love, she broke down and started crying. After she regained her composure, everybody walked her over to a big cake with her face on it and the two sweetest words: WELCOME HOME.

Before Saleena could blow out the candle, Rimzy decided to drop a jewel. "A wise person once said, 'the more you know, the less you realize you know.' I'm going to add on by saying I want you to know that the fam is forever. Saleena, we love you, we missed you, and we'll always be here for you. Welcome home."

"It feels good to be home," Saleena said, and then blew out the candle.

Chapter 28

Lieutenant Duwit didn't know how to react when he was summoned by police commissioner himself for a 9am meeting. He sat frigid in the impressive office not knowing whether he was facing praise or reprimand. As the commissioner entered, Duwit stood and attempted to offer pleasantries, but was met with a cold menacing stare. Duwit opened his mouth in some failed attempt to inquire about the reasoning for the impromptu meeting, but the commissioner spoke first, "What sort of idiot do you take me for, Duwit?" Worried and confused the lieutenant was only able to whisper a pathetic, "Sir?"

"Don't think that I'm not on to you and your goons," the commissioner fired back. "I got so much dirt on you that I could lose you in the system." With that said he pulled out a folder and slid it over to Duwit, "You are a very lucky man. They say timing is the key to most major moves. Since I'm coming up for re-election, taking you and your team down at this particular time would shine a very unfavorable light on my administration. So what I'm going to do is allow you to scrape by until my reelection. Your incompetent ass will sit in a squad car all day and give out fucking parking tickets until I can get rid of you without risking my campaign. But as soon as my seat is safely mine for another term, you better offer your resignation effective immediately, pack up your shit, AND GET THE FUCK OUT OF MY STATE!" the commissioner roared only inches away form lieutenant Duwit' face. "If I hear your name come up in anything I can guarantee you a nice long extended stay at Levenworth. Bottom line is your regime is over."

* * * * * *

Lieutenant Duwit was in a world of thought on his way home. Unable to focus, he pulled his car over and opened the file that held the answer to his questions.

Within the first few pages he found paperwork linking him to the Russian Mafia. As he read further, he discovered that all of their dealings had been sent back to the department. His mind raced trying to figure out how or why the Mafia would have sent such sensitive information exposing both himself and their organization to authorities.

He was the one who put the mob on to the Browns six months ago. He assured them that extorting the family would be like taking candy from a baby. He read further and realized that his vendetta against the Browns was now taking over his life. In the documents describing his Mafia involvement there was a note from the investigator on the case describing how peculiar it was that all of the records linking Duwit to the Russian Mob were sent four months after all of the Russian Mob bosses were murdered. Duwit figured out that one of them must have had some type of delayed, if anything happens to them booby-trap that exposed Duwits illegal operations.

When Duwit arranged for the Russians to target the Browns it never crossed his mind that they could take down the mob. Now he realized that he largely overestimated the power of the organization in which he placed his faith, because not only did the Browns demolish the mob, but someone in the family was even shrewd enough to sell him out to the commissioner; sending the intimate details of their dealings in to the department.

Duwit felt a burning sensation in his chest as the pain of his indiscretion set in. "I should have never dealt with those fucking incompetent Russians!" he yelled to himself. Through his hatred he managed to picture his son and was quelled for a moment. *It was all for my son*, he thought to himself. Lieutenant Duwit' son was the centerpiece of this entire debacle.

Rimzy's oldest brother, Jackson, killed Lieutenant Duwit' son. Duwit had been a dirty cop for many years. He had accumulated 30 kilos of cocaine for his own proprietorship. His son found the stash and tried to make a move with 10 kilos. Jackson who was also heavily into the drug game caught wind of the lightweight trying to come off and decided to take advantage. He robbed and murdered Duwit' son. Duwit was shocked to find out that his coke was missing and his son dead. One of his informants put him on to Jackson who was all of a sudden selling kilos for crazy low prices. It didn't take long for Duwit to put the pieces together realizing who killed his son, and consequently having Jackson killed.

Duwit thought that he had ended the situation when he ordered the successful hit on Jackson, but he was surprised when the youngest Brown brother, Ramel, found out who did the hit and murdered both of them. Duwit didn't like feeling tested and backed into a corner, so he embarked on a new mission to have Ramel buried under the jail. He took on the case and attempted to gain retribution through the legal system by setting up witnesses to testify againts Ramel in court with phony facts. His plan succeeded and Ramel was sent to jail for murder.

Duwit was willing to let everything go when Ramel came home, because he was in hot water with internal affairs. But when Ramel killed the witness enough was enough. Knowing that the matriarch is usually the person who's name is used to clean and hold the dirty money in legal institutions, Duwit enlisted the help of a department friend, who pulled up Rimzy's mother's finances. Low and behold he found that the mother owned a house and a plaza full of stores. He instantly came up with the plan to take down the remaining Browns' along with their home and plaza. However, his plan was failing miserably. With the Russians under the table he started to focus on Rimzy. He he decided that before he 'packed his shit,' as the commissioner demanded, he had to make sure Rimzy wasn't the cause of his downfall. With a new target set, Duwit put his car in drive, and proceeded home. All of this was going through his head as he pulled into his driveway.

Chapter 29

Things started out smoothly on October 5th, until Rimzy got a phone call that left him utterly speechless.

"Excuse me, Mr. Brown?"

Rimzy saw the number had a Texas area code, and the only people he knew out there were the boys. Rimzy instantly got a funny feeling.

"Yes," he responded hesitantly.

"I'm Lieutenant Malcot from the County Sheriff's Department. I'm afraid I have some very bad news."

Rimzy's heart started pumping one-hundred miles an hour. Something was seriously wrong.

"Yes?" Rimzy said.

"I regret to inform you that Mrs. Johnson and her husband were in a very bad automobile accident that resulted in their demise. It was brought to our attention that Geovoni and Geavonté are your biological children. Can you confirm that you are actually their father?"

"Yes, I'm the twin's father," he replied, feeling numb.

"Okay, I'm going to transfer you over to our child development department at Social Services. Just hold on one second."

Rimzy heard the click as the lieutenant transferred lines. After about two minutes, the lieutenant clicked back over.

"Hello, Mr. Brown?"

"Yes?"

"I have Mrs. Crawford on the line. She will take it from here. Sorry about your loss."

Mrs. Crawford spoke, "First, my entire department and I send our regards to you and your family. We've already verified, through department of records, that you are the twin's biological father. You are the twin's only kin that we can trace. So, I need to know if you're going to make arrangements to come and get the boys."

"As soon as I get off the phone with you, I'll be making arrangements."

Arrangements? Rimzy thought, *It sounds like they are trying to move furniture.*

"Now, before I get all of the information from you, could I speak to the twins?"

"I have no problem with that," Mrs. Crawford replied, "but I must advise you that because of the boys' ages, we have not told them what happened. The courts decided that if the next of kin could be located within a certain amount of time, they would tell the children."

"How long have you had the boys?"

"We picked them up at precisely nine o'clock last night."

Rimzy glanced down at his watch. It was 11 a.m., which meant fourteen hours had passed.

"They haven't transferred to a housing unit as of yet. After all the paperwork is done, which will be within the next hour, they will be moved. Okay, here are the boys. They each have a phone, so you'll be talking to them simultaneously."

Both boys spoke in unison. "Dad?"

"Yes, it's me. Listen, I'm trying to get a flight out there as soon as time allows to come see you."

"Dad, why can't Mom come get us?" Geovoni asked. "What's going on? Why are we in here? I want to go home." Every sentence

Geovoni spoke, his tone became more harsh and loud. By the time he spoke the last sentence he was roaring.

"Listen to me. I'll answer all of your questions when I get there. In the meantime, both of you stick together like glue. You watch each other's backs. I'll be there before you know it. So breathe easy until I get there. How are the people treating you in there?"

This time, Geovonté spoke. "They are being very nice, but they're not answering us when we ask them any questions about Mom."

"Don't worry about a thing. I'll be there. Until then, just stay strong and hold each other down. Okay?"

There was a short silence before they both answered in unison. "Okay, Dad."

After writing down all the information Mrs. Crawford gave him, Rimzy hung the phone up in a daze. He immediately called Blue.

"Listen, I need you to do me a really big favor. I need to be on the next available flight to Texas. I need to make a few calls to cancel an appointment, so hit me back with my flight information ASAP."

Rimzy was supposed to look at a plot of land with his land surveyor, so he had to make three calls in order to reschedule.

Rimzy's private phone started ringing as soon as he finished rescheduling; it was Blue again. "I have a flight for this afternoon at three o'clock out of JFK. Is that good for you? If so, I can book it right now."

"Book it." At that precise moment, another call came through. "I'll call you back for the confirmation number. Thank you." With that said, he clicked over to wifey. "Hey, love."

"Baby, it's time."

Rimzy responded, "Well, you know the routine Sanae. I'll be there in about twenty minutes."

"No, my water just broke. Hurry up, baby."

"I'm there." As he hung up the phone, he thought, *what are the odds of these two events happening at the same time?*

He concluded that some type of higher force was testing him and he had to rise to the occasion.

Rimzy was on Houston and Broadway, so it was nothing for him to cut across town, jump on the Westside highway, and zoom to the Bronx. There were lights on the highway up until 59th Street, so he couldn't burn it up the way he wanted. However, once he reached the elevated portion of the highway, he aired it out. He was whipping over one-hundred miles an hour all the way up town.

By the time Rimzy pulled up if front of the house, wifey was waiting out front with the bag they already had packed and ready to go. Soon as the car stopped, Rimzy jumped out of the vehicle, ran over to her, kissed her, walked her over to the door, opened it, and shut it as she reclined in the seat. As soon as Sanae was situated in the passenger seat, Rimzy got in, started the engine and took off. He zoomed right by the black impala that was parked on the corner, totally unaware of who sat watching his every move inside.

Lieutenant Duwit felt the excitement bubble up inside of him. He had been stalking Rimzy nonstop ever since he was scolded by the commissioner. He had sat for weeks waiting for the opportunity to take him down. Duwit waited for Rimzy to pass, and then followed him, not sure of where they were headed but certain that this was his chance to settle his vendetta.

In no time, Rimzy was zooming through the E-Z pass lane, which led to Manhattan. After a few loops, he was on the George Washington Bridge. There was a lot of traffic on the turnpike and they had to go to exit 14, the Newark Airport exit.

It was a no brainer. Rimzy went all the way to the left and was flying eighty miles an hour in the emergency lane. Rimzy knew it was going to be a hard push going to Newark, but wifey had insisted that the family physician deliver the baby, and she was based out of Newark. So, Newark it was.

Everything was going smooth until an unmarked police cruiser pulled up behind them, sirens blaring. Rimzy paid him no mind for about a mile. The officer was screaming at Rimzy through the bullhorn to pull over.

Sanae looked over and asked, "Why don't you pull over and explain the situation?"

"Fuck the police! We can talk it out in front of the hospital."

They drove like that for about three miles before another driver cut Rimzy off causing him to jam the breaks, just grazing the other car's bumper and forcing a confrontation. As soon as the cars came to a stop, the cop followed suit, then jumped out of his vehicle like a mad man, with his gun drawn.

All the rage Lieutenant Duwit felt swelled up out of control and redirected itself toward Rimzy. He hit the switch that activated the lights and siren. Lieutenant Duwit couldn't believe Rimzy was ignoring his identity and making him chase him down like a dog.

Rimzy made out Lieutenant Duwit immediately and definitely didn't like the look in the officer's eyes or his body language as he approached the car. He looked over, and in a stern voice, he told Sanae, "Do not get out of the car no matter what."

With that said, Rimzy got out, hands up and in front of him, to try to help defuse the situation. Although he recognized Lieutenant Duwit Rimzy didn't let on for Sanae's sake. The last thing he wanted was this confrontation while his son's were stranded in Texas and wifey was ready to give birth. Rimzy decided to play dumb with officer Duwit. "Listen, my wife is having a baby right now, and…"

Lieutenant Duwit cut him off, not hearing a word he said. "Shut up and lay face down on the ground!"

Rimzy flatly refused. "NO!"

Lieutenant Duwit started getting nervous. He never encountered a situation where he had his gun drawn and someone refused his authority. Lieutenant Duwit yelled his command a little louder and firmer. "I'm going to ask you one more time. Lay down on the ground."

Rimzy's adrenaline was through the roof. It was all happing so fast; yet it seemed like it was moving in slow motion. Lieutenant Duwit was a certified third-degree black belt. As he inched closer, he lashed out and kicked Rimzy in the solar plexus.

As Rimzy was falling back, he saw a blur as Lieutenant Duwit kicked him on the side of his head. Rimzy dropped to one knee and put one hand in the air as an act of submission. Rimzy put his other hand on the floor to balance himself. He was a little dazed, but he acted much more hurt than he was.

Lieutenant Duwit disregarded Rimzy's hand in the air and spun around to catch him with a full roundhouse. As he was in the air, Rimzy lunged forward, caught the Lieutenant's leg, and used Duwit' momentum to help slam him on his face.

Rimzy knew he didn't have any wins trying to fight this cop straight up. He had to find an angle. He knew the officer had a lot of malice by the look on his face. Rimzy acted like he was more hurt than he was hoping that the officer would slip up, and that's exactly what he did.

Lieutenant Duwit was obviously in a daze as he tried to pick himself up off of the ground. Rimzy was not going to give him the opportunity to regain his composure. He was about to rush the officer, when suddenly someone grabbed him from behind and wrapped him up in a bear hug. It was the driver of the car which Rimzy grazed. Confused by the scuffle the other driver thought that Rimzy was attempting to beat up a police officer and tried to act as a Good Samaritan. While Rimzy was struggling to get free, Lieutenant Duwit had the time he needed to dig into his ankle holster and pull out his .380.

When Duwit got slammed on his face, his Glock fell out of his hand into the roadway. His vision was a little blurry, but not blurry enough to miss the two figures that seemed to be advancing on him. Without thinking twice, he blindly fired nine shots in the direction of the figures.

The so-called Good Samaritan's wife and two children watched in disbelief as their father fell to the ground. Out of the nine shots, six of them found their mark. Five hit Rimzy, all body shots. The so-called Good Samaritan got hit once in the head and died instantly. Rimzy was on the ground in convulsions as Lieutenant Duwit approached. By now, the two wives were out of the cars crying hysterically.

"Why? Why? Why?" Sanae yelled. "He did nothing wrong! We were speeding because I'm in labor! His only crime was rushing me to the hospital to have our baby! Why? Why? Why?"

Then Sanae fell out, as the sound of sirens could be heard in the distance.

www.NewYorkStateOfMindBook.com